UNCIVIL RIGHTS

e
ged
ight

Bilingual Press/Editorial Bilingüe

General Editor
Gary D. Keller

Managing Editor
Karen S. Van Hooft

Associate Editors
Karen M. Akins
Barbara H. Firoozye

Assistant Editor
Linda St. George Thurston

Editorial Board
Juan Goytisolo
Francisco Jiménez
Eduardo Rivera
Mario Vargas Llosa

Address:
Bilingual Press
Hispanic Research Center
Arizona State University
P.O. Box 872702
Tempe, Arizona 85287-2702
(602) 965-3867

UNCIVIL RIGHTS

AND OTHER STORIES

Nash Candelaria

Bilingual Press/Editorial Bilingüe
TEMPE, ARIZONA

ISBN 0-927534-83-5

Library of Congress Cataloging-in-Publication Data

Candelaria, Nash.
    Uncivil rights and other stories / Nash Candelaria.
       p.   cm.
    Contents: Uncivil rights — The dancing school — A whole lot of justice — Dear Rosita — The border — Family Thanksgiving — Radio waves.
    ISBN 0-927534-83-5 (alk. paper)
    1. Mexican-Americans—Social life and customs—Fiction. I. Title.
PS3553.A4896U53   1998
813'.54—dc21   98-35871
                                                CIP

PRINTED IN THE UNITED STATES OF AMERICA

Back cover photo by Michael Collopy
Cover design, interior by John Wincek, Aerocraft Charter Art Service

Acknowledgments

Partial funding provided by the Arizona Commission on the Arts through appropriations from the Arizona State Legislature and grants from the National Endowment for the Arts.

"Dear Rosita" is reprinted with permission from the publisher of *The Americas Review,* Vol. 19, No.2 (Houston: Arte Público Press—University of Houston, 1994).

"Family Council," which forms a portion of "Uncivil Rights," is reprinted with permission from the publisher of *The Americas Review,* Vol. 22, Nos. 1-2 (Houston: Arte Público Press—University of Houston, 1994).

The following appeared in previous publications: "Family Thanksgiving," in *Mirrors Beneath the Earth*, ed. Ray González (Willimantic, CT: Curbstone Press, 1992). "Radio Waves," in *Imagine*, Volume II, No. 2 (Winter 1985), 41-46. "The Dancing School," in *The Bilingual Review/La Revista Bilingüe,* Volume 17, No. 3 (September-December 1992), 256-263. "A Whole Lot of Justice," in *The Bilingual Review/La Revista Bilingüe,* Volume 20, No. 1 (January-April 1995), 45-52. "The Border," in *The Bilingual Review/La Revista Bilingüe,* Volume 21, No. 3 (September-December 1996), 241-253.

CONTENTS

By Nash Candelaria

Novels:

Memories of the Alhambra
Not by the Sword
Inheritance of Strangers
Leonor Park

Short Stories:

The Day the Cisco Kid Shot John Wayne

UNCIVIL RIGHTS

Alfonso Peña was a wrinkle of a man. Not just the creases around his eyes, the corners of his mouth, or his neck. Not just his clothes. But everything about him. His life was an unneat series of furrows and rumples that were chaotic and irretrievably fixed. No iron was hot enough, no steam press powerful enough to smooth them out.

Even more than that, his soul was a wrinkle. An unevenness of hills and valleys that added up to confusion and chaos. It was seldom anything big that undid him. No capital sin damned him forever. No felony caused him to be locked up where they'd throw away the key. It was an accumulation of little sins, a swamp of veniality, that held him back. That kept him from moving toward anything—anything at all. His life was a mess. A pair of muddy shoes that left its tracks everywhere.

This particular day he had taken the bus from his little adobe house in the farming suburb of Los Rafas into the city of Albuquerque. His car was not running, and he did not have the money to have it repaired. He had told his wife that he was going into town for a job interview, which was a lie. Alfonso did not have the courage nor the revolver to hold up banks, so a job it would have to be—sometime. Not that he wouldn't engage in a minor case of larceny if the opportunity presented itself.

He stumbled off the bus in the old downtown section of Central Avenue that was being renovated. He sidled up alertly behind a man retrieving the morning newspaper from a vending machine. When the man turned with newspaper in hand, Alfonso quickly caught the cover before it slammed shut.

Now, he thought, he could at least search the classified advertising in case his wife should question him. Since he preferred to read the newspaper in comfort, habit led him toward a coffee shop that he and fellow workers had frequented before he had been fired from the advertising agency. Alfonso had the hopeful feeling that someone he knew would be there and would pick up the tab for a hot cup and a sweet roll.

It was not to be. The place was empty except for the paisano behind the counter. "Hey," the waiter said in Spanish. "Haven't seen you in months. You still at the same place?"

Why was it, Alfonso thought, that the help never showed proper respect? If there had been others in the shop he would have ignored the question, pretending that he had not heard it.

"I'm freelancing," he said without thinking. It was, he suddenly realized, an avenue he had not pursued for some time.

Even in a city of nearly half a million people the advertising community was a relatively small one. He was known by many with whom he had had falling-outs over one thing or another, parting with bitter feelings. And the word travelled fast, even to those he didn't know.

They were fools, he told himself. So-called art directors and advertising managers with little taste and less talent. That was the price one paid for working with fools. They didn't recognize good art when they saw it. They refused to pay the price for first-class work. Then they bad-mouthed you to others in the business.

This reputation had been his undoing during the reference checks that followed hopeful job interviews. Later there were no interviews, even after repeated calls, as if his reputation had preceded him.

"It's the fucking system," he mumbled. "A goddamned conspiracy."

"What's that?" the waiter asked.

"Nothing. Nothing."

The fucking fat cats, he thought. Sucking money from the working man, then not giving him a chance to work. They don't do that to you in Cuba. There everybody works. Everybody eats. Everybody shares. What we need is a good revolution. Then we'll see how these rich, powerful pigs like it when they have to live on slop and bed down in outhouses.

"So," the waiter said. "What kind of freelancing do you do?"

"Art!" His voice burst out, almost a shout, filled with anger and frustration. His hands moved away from each other, hesitated, then moved out again. "Big art! Too good for the advertising business."

"Must be a lotta money in that."

"I'm a fucking millionaire. Now come on. Give me another cup of coffee."

The waiter's mouth fell open. He filled Alfonso's cup, then turned and retreated to the end of the counter, wiping the already clean top.

First they steal your country, Alfonso thought. Then they steal your language so you can't even think naturally. You think in gringo. Then, when you can't or won't talk gringo, they call you stupid. Estúpidos don't deserve jobs. All they deserve is a kick in the ass. When you decide a sore ass is no substitute for a full belly and you complain, they call you a troublemaker and haul you off to jail.

He grabbed at his stomach, the cold pain shooting through him like an icicle. Then the icicle reached out with frozen tentacles that squeezed and shook his insides. His forehead broke out in sweat. He closed his eyes and grimaced.

The waiter had finally worked his way back along the counter. "Hey, you all right, man?"

"My goddamned ulcer. That's what advertising does to you." Which, like so much of what Alfonso said, was not an outright lie but was not the whole truth, either. For he often thought that he was born with the damned thing. Not enough chichi when he was a baby. And a poor man couldn't always afford milk to soothe an aching stomach. Christ!

True, he was living in his dead mother's house rent free. Well, almost rent free. His goddamned brother and sister wanted him to pay something. All three of them had inherited the house equally. But Christ, they had homes. Nice homes. Not some tiny hundred-year-old adobe farmhouse that started to dissolve when the humidity went up. Pretty soon he and his wife would be living inside transparent walls while the air outside would turn dirt brown from dissolving adobe.

Anyway—Shit! he said to himself, interrupting his train of thought. He should forget the goddamned newspaper and its want ads and take the bus to the university law library. Then he'd teach that money-grubbing brother and sister of his a thing or two. They had no right to kick him out. The house was as much his as theirs. Where would he and Dolores live? In the street? Was that what it had come to?

He stared at the cup of coffee, considering whether or not to push it aside and move on to the bus stop. Impulsively, he reached instead for the pitcher of thin blue milk that passed for coffee cream and filled the empty half of his cup. There. That would help his stomach. The beginning of a milk diet. Settle down, he said silently to his innards. I'm feeding you just like a baby.

Meanwhile, the waiter had been watching him as if expecting a collapse or a fit. But the pain passed, and Alfonso's color returned.

"You think you got troubles," the waiter said, nodding toward the newspaper beside Alfonso's cup. "What about that priest, Father Ted? We used to go to that parish. North of here across the river. Even God doesn't protect you any more."

Priest and Cohorts Indicted for Alien Smuggling, the headline read.

Alfonso unfolded the paper and glanced at the photograph of a stocky priest; a middle-aged, heavyset woman; a tall, gray-haired man in a business suit; and a slender young woman between two Federal cops. A nice-looking woman in a dark suit was talking to the priest. They meant nothing to Alfonso.

"Irene Bustamante," he read. "Federal Public Defender—" The name was familiar. But then, hell, the city was full of Bustamantes. His poor dead mother's sister had married a Bustamante.

He looked up and saw the waiter watching him. "Yeah," the waiter said. "He can't afford a real lawyer so they give him this woman lawyer. From an old family around here."

"Everybody's old family around here," Alfonso said. "Nobody has enough sense to get the hell out of this rat hole."

But inside he felt a surge of excitement. Daniel, he remembered. Cousin Daniel. That lawyer must be his daughter. He remembered years ago, when he and Daniel were still speaking, the happy toddler who had driven him crazy busybodying all over the room as if nothing could keep her still. Little Reeny.

He stared at the newspaper, clouds of vague thought coalescing.

* * *

"I can have a thousand protesters surrounding the federal courthouse at an hour's notice!" Alfonso gripped the telephone as if it was a policeman's throat. "You think they're going to ignore that? Hell! Who do you think was behind the protests during the Bicentennial? The photograph of that sign that was in all the newspapers: THEY CAME TO REMIND US THAT WE ARE A CONQUERED PEOPLE! Remember that? All you have to do is remind the goddamned power structure that the real power is in the people. They'll crap their pants. They can't fight the will of the people."

Alfonso could tell from her tone of voice that she was resisting. First of all, she was probably wondering who he was even though he had told her that her father's mother and his mother were sisters, both bearers of the proud name of Baca. Historic people. Among the conquistadors that tamed this ass-hole country. But then, what did people know about history, especially their own history? Especially nowadays. They didn't know shit.

Maybe he should have toned down his language, except that it was too late for that. When he had telephoned the office some snotty-voiced woman said that Ms. Bustamante was in conference and couldn't be disturbed. Could he leave his num-ber so she could call him back? Except that Alfonso had been that route too many times, waiting for calls that never came. No, thank you. He'd hold on the line.

"Tell her it's her cousin," he had insisted. "Tell her it's important. A matter of cultural pride."

When Ms. Bustamante finally came to the telephone, sound-ing even snottier than the first woman, he had waited so long that he couldn't control his language. It flowed vehemently, gathering force with every word, an avalanche of insistence that would not stop for fear that he would be rejected again.

Finally Alfonso heaved a sigh—that is, exhaled the smoke from the fire that burned inside him. He stared out of the fly-specked glass of the telephone booth. The pharmacist was talking to a short, round, dark woman who held a slip of paper tightly in her right hand. Two other customers stood in line behind her, poor paisanos who lived in the neighborhood.

He looked out the window of the drugstore. It was a small place compared to those in the newer parts of town. Across the potholed street lay an empty lot, dry, dusty, and forlorn. Three young men stood in front of the store as if they had no better place to be, cigarettes dangling from their lips. They turned in unison, bobbing their heads in greeting at a passing lowrider.

Ms. Bustamante's grandfather, Alfonso's Uncle Matías, had scraped a livelihood from his worthless mountain acres by sell-ing firewood door-to-door from an old Ford truck. As a treat, old Uncle Matías would occasionally take Alfonso and his cousin Daniel up in the mountains to pick piñon. The boys would race to see who could fill their gunnysacks with the most pine nuts. Later they would sell their bounty to one of the tienditas in town not unlike this crummy old drugstore. Now, talking to Ms. Bustamante reminded him that his cousin Daniel had been dead for a dozen years—he had forgotten about that—and that he, Alfonso, was no longer a boy.

"We can't have that, Señor Peña! That would make matters worse!" She sounded like his sister bitching at him about something—anything.

But he couldn't help himself. On he rambled, his voice rising toward hysteria, not sure what he was saying except that he had to make her understand. Understand what? He wasn't sure of that either.

"What is it exactly that you want, Señor Peña?" She spoke in Spanish this time, the unguarded language of intimacy among brown-skinned New Mexicans, especially among family. Except that there wasn't a hint of intimacy in her voice. It was a voice tainted with accusation. A voice talking to someone who was an embarrassment. A voice talking in the presence of foreigners who did not understand Spanish and who the voice hoped would not notice.

"I read about the sanctuary people," Alfonso said. "About what the fucking government is trying to do to them. I been through that. Ask me about 1976. About the teachers' union. They fired me for speaking up for my rights."

There was silence from the other end of the line, a silence of disapproval, as if she had just sniffed something abominably foul. "There is a team of lawyers representing them," Ms. Bustamante finally said. "Are you a lawyer?"

Peña felt his eyes strain, the skin on his face tighten. But even more, Peña felt his anger rising. She must have known damned well that he was no lawyer. He resented her uncivil rejection. Back in 1976, when he had been a mover and shaker in the Movimiento, people were clamoring for his help.

"Look," she continued. "I'm extremely busy. I have some-body at my desk waiting to talk to me. What is it that you want?" When he didn't answer right away, her voice softened. "I think I remember you from your mother's funeral. My grandmother and I went to the services. I was truly sorry that your mother and my grandmother drifted apart over the years. Sisters should stick together."

At least, Alfonso thought, she didn't ask me why I wasn't at her father's funeral. "Look," he said. "I can get a thousand picketers out like that—" He snapped his fingers. "The judge will get the picture. Just tell me, and I'll round up the faithful from the Movement. They can't do that to innocent people. To the priest. To you."

"No, thank you! I have enough worries without someone starting a riot in front of the federal courthouse. The defen-dants' problems are in the hands of their lawyers and the justice system. If you want to help, don't even think about protests."

Justice system! In disgust, Alfonso cleared his throat and spat onto the floor of the telephone booth. For an instant he regretted that he had shot off his mouth. Some people wouldn't recognize how to get things done if you stuck it up their ass. The hell with it!

"I gotta go," Alfonso said abruptly. "I got a job interview over near Old Town. If you don't want my help—" He shrugged and hung up, cutting her off in mid sentence. Then he walked out into the clear, sunny morning and headed toward the bus stop.

* * *

The gentle sway of the bus and the warm desert sun lulled Alfonso into a state of drowsiness. He was grateful for small favors. Talking to his cousin Daniel's daughter had reawakened memories. He had forgotten that the man had been dead the past twelve years, that he had died about the time Alfonso was in the midst of his troubles with the school administration.

And Daniel's mother was still alive, while her sister, Alfonso's mother, was rotting in the ground.

It had been a year since Mamá had passed away. The memory of her death carried a heavy load of regret, remorse, and anger. The last time he had seen his mother alive was in the hospital. At that stage of her illness she had been in the intensive care ward, tubes sticking into her nose, needles in her arm, some strange electronic machine blinking traces across the face of a tiny screen: Channel Death.

"The nurse said she's a little better today," his brother Cipriano had whispered when he had sidled in. His sister Margarita had tossed him a look, eyebrow lifted, without saying what Alfonso knew she was thinking: Late as usual.

Alfonso had looked down at the old woman on the bed. Her eyes were closed, but he could sense that she was listening. The gray, thinning hair was bunched up where her head rested on the pillow. A few strands were matted against her forehead, and her mouth hung slack as if she could not control it, as if she had had a stroke. But it had not been a stroke. It was cancer. Cancer of the pancreas. Incurable and just a matter of time.

"I couldn't get off work," Alfonso said in a stage whisper. Although he was looking at Cipriano, he had meant it for Margarita.

"The sons-a-bitches," he continued. "I could be dying of a heart attack, and they'd shove a pencil in my hand for one last drawing."

Margarita shook her head. "Shh—," she said, meaning his cursing. "The priest was just here." Then she added, almost in tears, "Poor Mamá. She looks so weak. God—" shaking her head. "God."

The not-yet corpse stirred and emitted a low groan. But Alfonso had his mind on other things. "What'd she say about the house?" he whispered. "Did she say anything about the house?"

After that he didn't remember exactly what had happened. He had been too intent on his own needs. Too intent on making sure that he didn't get screwed by Margarita and Cipriano, who were bad influences on his mother. It seemed that everything he did was twisted into some form of accusation that drove the old lady into a frenzy.

It might have been that Margarita told him, "Shh," one time too many. Or that like so often, she had started to pray aloud, asking them to join in, although Alfonso knew she meant it mostly for him. Well, if he wanted to pray he would have gone to goddamned church. Who the hell was she? Some kind of nun?

Maybe Cipriano had told him to shut up because Mamá could hear. Couldn't Alfonso see that the dear thing was trying to speak? That the slack lips tightened as if trying to form words? Then Cipriano would have taken the old lady's hand to show that he cared. To show that he was the good son. The kiss-ass good son. "Mamá, I love you more than anyone." Mierda!

Or maybe—no. It couldn't have been what Alfonso might have said. He wasn't that insensitive. Arguing over the little adobe house in the intensive care ward. That's what Margarita and Cipriano would say now. But they would have said that no matter what. They were always ganging up on him. He, little brother Alfonso, the black sheep.

Whatever—he couldn't remember now. Except that suddenly like one of those horror movies where the corpse opens its eyes and points a shaking finger in accusation—the old lady raised her head off the pillow. "How dare you," she had croaked at Alfonso. "Get out! Don't come back. You didn't let me live in peace. Now, for God's sakes, let me die in peace!"

He had been shocked. Mamá hadn't really meant it. She was sick. She didn't know what she was saying. Margarita had put Mamá up to it. Who knows what stories that bitch sister of his had been telling the old lady?

Out! He remembered the trembling finger, the tubes dangling from her arm like some obscene plastic rosary, the look of hate on the old lady's face. Out!

When he had tried to reach for her, to take her hand and calm her down, Cipriano had gotten between them. "You better go," he had hissed. "Can't you see how you've upset her? Jesus Christ, Fonso. When are you ever going to learn?"

"Well, fuck you!" he had said aloud. "She's my mother too. Fuck all of you!"

Then out. Bumping into the doctor as he stormed down the hall. "She's my mother too!" he had shouted at the doctor who had looked at him in surprise.

That was the last he had seen the old lady alive. The next time it had been at the funeral parlor. The coffin lid open. Mamá in her Sunday black dress that differed from the black dresses she wore during the week only in that it was newer and better made. He couldn't remember seeing her in anything other than black since his father had died. Back when he was in high school. Just before he had gone into the army.

"Listen, Mamá," he had said to the still, waxlike corpse that somewhat resembled Mamá but was not really her. "Listen," he said, instead of the prayers that others at the coffin mumbled under their breaths. "You didn't mean what you said in the hospital. I know that. I know you loved me. And I want to tell you that I'm not angry. I know you weren't yourself. I know that Margarita poisoned your mind with lies about me. I forgive you, Mamá, and I pray for you every day."

Still thinking those thoughts while the priest droned through the church service and then over the open grave. Still thinking when the funeral attendees made their way to Margarita's house for the obligatory after-funeral get-together.

Margarita ran around to everybody, accepting their embraces and giving them her tears in return. In between she went back and forth to the kitchen with the hot casseroles that people had brought. Acting more like the goddamned hostess at a coming-out party than the grieving daughter of the departed.

Well, Alfonso had thought, she was my mother too. And he accepted the condolences of those who came. Some of whom were wary, not having seen Alfonso for years. Having heard about his troubles years ago but acting as if they had been yesterday. About his militancy. Getting fired from his teaching job. Having his photograph spread across the front page of the newspapers. Leading a protest that had erupted into the shooting of some poor paisano by the police.

Through the dreariness of the gathering he tried to remain solemn. Not that he did not feel the sadness, the loss. For in truth, during all his troubles over the years, the troubles that many of the people gathered here remembered too well, it had been his mother who had stood behind him. He knew that no matter how angry she had been, she had never really meant that anger. That he had been her favorite. He had been the one who had come around most often, even though many times it was to ask for money.

But through the dreary gathering, dry-eyed, ready to scream, he could only sense the unreality of it all. The subdued cocktail party atmosphere. The sad way some people looked at him yet avoided him if they could. His unbelievable, uncontrollable feeling that he would burst into laughter if one more person turned away from him and rushed toward Margarita or Cipriano.

Then, after all that draining intensity, there had been the heightened expectation when the will was read a few days later. He should have known what would happen. He knew what bloodsuckers lawyers were.

But there it was, Mamá's words coming out of that cold-fish lawyer who rushed through the reading, in a hurry to collect his fee. "My house and all my worldly goods, except for the small bequest to the Church of the Immaculate Heart, I give equally to my son Cipriano and my daughter Margarita. My son Alfonso has received more than his share during my lifetime. All I can leave him now are my fervent prayers that he will mend his ways before it is too late."

The shock! At least Margarita had the good grace not to snicker. Cipriano had avoided looking at him. Disinherited!

Left nothing. Not a dirty adobe brick or a single raw frijol. Jesus! He had almost collapsed right there. Now what the hell was he going to do?

If you had only known the truth, Mamá, he thought as the bus approached the old center of the city. If you hadn't listened to other people's lies.

He looked alertly out the window. They were approaching the building where Cipriano had his barber shop—no, now it was a hair salon. Fancy. Alfonso stared to make sure that it was still there on the wall. The huge, spray-can painted graffiti. Garamond bold he had made it. Worthy of the finest typesetter. In black against the desert tan of the building. "Cipriano Peña is a capitalist marrano!"

Alfonso couldn't help but smile. It was still there. They'd have to sandblast the building to get it off. His brother was too cheap to do that.

Very nice, Alfonso thought. Not only artistic but literary too. "Capitalistic marrano!" Hah. Marrano was Spanish for pig. But what pleased him most was not the bilingualism of it. Hell, even the Anglos around here knew a little Spanish. It was the double meaning of marrano, a literary allusion or whatever the hell they called it. Because marrano had another meaning, one that went way back to when his ancestors had first settled this miserable place in the seventeenth century. A marrano referred to a Jew who ate pork. That is, a Jew who had forsaken his faith to save his life during the Spanish Inquisition. Who knows what money-grubbing strain might have sneaked into the family, especially into Cipriano, who was a capitalistic marrano. A pig. A Jew. Both.

A departing passenger left behind a folded tangle of newspaper. Alfonso moved quickly and grabbed it. When he looked out the window he saw that the bus was alongside the old Kimo Theater.

"Transfer," he demanded of the driver. Then he hopped off, slapping the folded newspaper against his thigh. A new idea had occurred to him.

* * *

"I'm sorry," the blond receptionist said after the third attempt to get through. "Her line is still busy."

"I'm her cousin," Alfonso said. "It's very important that I talk to her."

She flashed a weak smile that was not even a good pretense. He could tell that she wanted him to leave. The hell with her, Alfonso thought. He headed past the reception counter toward the door into the interior of the building.

"Sir!" The receptionist's voice rose in alarm. "Sir! You can't go in there."

Two visitors, looking uncomfortable in their neat but unstylish clothes, looked up from the government issue chairs on which they sat. The receptionist quickly tapped a succession of pushbuttons on her telephone.

Alfonso half expected a siren to scream. As he put his hand on the doorknob he realized that if he continued they would probably throw him out. He would have no chance of speaking to Ms. Bustamante.

He sighed and turned back toward the counter, ignoring the nervous stares of the waiting visitors. Jailbirds, he thought. That's what they look like. Tarted up so their free lawyers might think they're innocent.

Before he was halfway to the counter the door popped open and a uniformed marshal walked out, scanning left and right like he was walking a beat in a tough barrio. The marshal's hand was on his left hip over the small rectangular holster that housed a walkie-talkie.

Here it comes, Alfonso thought. He looked down at his rumpled trousers and the poor excuse for a sport coat. He tried to adjust his necktie that he had loosened while on the bus. At least he had shaved this morning. But deep inside he was prepared for rejection, thinking that if he was in a pressed business suit or was white-skinned, he would be treated differently.

He was trying to decide whether or not to make a scene as the marshal approached the counter. He could see the moving lips of the officer and the receptionist, but he couldn't hear the words. The marshal looked over his shoulder at Alfonso.

"I'll wait," Alfonso said, the closest he would ever come to an apology. The unexpected sound of his voice was like a shout in the uneasy quiet. He dropped onto a chair facing one of the visitors, who looked away.

The dark-complected marshal strolled across the lobby and leaned over Alfonso, speaking in Spanish. "Señor Peña, you want to talk to Attorney Bustamante? You'll have to wait until she's off the telephone. The receptionist is only doing her job. When I go back in I'll tell Ms. Bustamante that you're waiting."

The guard smiled a dark-brown, friendly smile that had an edge to it. I'll be nice if you don't fuck with me, it said.

Alfonso nodded, loosening his grip on the arms of the chair. Well, he thought, though still wary, that's more like it. He straightened his tie and tossed a glare toward the receptionist who was busy on the telephone. Then he smiled toward the visitor opposite, who still would not acknowledge him. This time Alfonso did not react, did not curse the man under his breath or give it another thought.

In a few minutes the door opened and a sturdy, good-looking young woman with a harried expression on her face walked to the counter. The receptionist nodded in Alfonso's direction. The woman approached rapidly, her dark eyes under thick black brows boring into him.

"Let's sit over there," she commanded. She did not say "away from the others" but Alfonso knew what she meant.

"What is it that you want?" she asked.

"Don't you recognize me?"

"No."

After his disappointment, Alfonso realized: Why should she? He didn't remember her from his mother's funeral. He had not been close to her father since high school. He had seen Daniel infrequently and mostly by accident until the time of his death. Their lives had taken different paths.

He vaguely remembered the overactive little girl who was Daniel's oldest daughter. He would not have recognized the woman she had become except for the captioned photograph in the newspaper. She was a celebrity now, a famous person.

"I'm your cousin Alfonso." Her expression did not change. "Alfonso Peña," he added, disappointed that she did not recognize his name.

She blinked and her face lit up with—with what?— amusement? suspicion? "Yes," she said. "The phone call. The radical."

Yes, Alfonso thought. The radical. The socialist. Defender of the poor. Fighter against bigotry. Champion of the brown-skinned and the red-skinned. Militant. Outspoken. Burr under the saddle of the powerful. Wielder of the custard pie against the pompous. Revealer of the emperor's clothes. Searchlight on the privileged and unfair. Troublemaker. Don Quixote de los Frijoles. What the hell did this young twit know?

"As I told you on the telephone, I want to help."

The expression on her face hardened. "I think my position on that was very clear."

"I have a daughter your age," he said. "Maybe a little younger. She lives in California."

What he didn't say was that he suspected that she had moved to get away from him. Lupe had never told him that outright, but he sensed it anyway. His wife had told him often enough to stop meddling in their daughter's life. Then Lupe had married this young Anglo engineer and gone away. Now there were only birthday and Christmas cards. Occasional telephone calls. Occasional visits on vacation.

Ms. Bustamante eyed him suspiciously. Her dark eyes made him uncomfortable, as if she could see deep inside him and know his most secret thoughts. She ignored his comment about his daughter.

"We have a team of lawyers working for us. What I really need right now is to get back to my desk and get on with my work."

"I've been through this kind of thing before," he said. "I know what these courts can do. Find innocent people guilty. See conspiracies where none exist. What the defendants need is popular support. A show that we Spanish-speaking people are not going to put up with their shit."

She stiffened and took a deep breath, her dark brows arching. No more cursing, he thought to himself. Bureaucrats do not like four-letter words.

"I can get a thousand people picketing the federal courthouse at an hour's notice," he said.

"No. Our lawyers are handling this. That's the last thing we want. Look," she said, "this conversation is getting nowhere. I can't stop you from doing whatever you want as long as it's within the law, but I think it's a bad idea. Now I have to go back to work."

Then again, unable to help himself, "I'm an artist. I want to draw the court proceedings and sell them to the newspapers. I—" He couldn't say it. Tell her that he desperately needed a job.

"I can't do anything about that," she said. "You can do anything you want in the courtroom as long as you don't disrupt the proceedings. As for the newspapers, talk to them." Then abruptly, "I can't talk anymore. I have to get back to my desk."

She turned and walked quickly away. She doesn't know what difficulties she's going to face in court, he thought. Thank God she has a relative who can be of service. Which for him was the equivalent of a promise.

*　*　*

The bus stopped across from the university. It was late afternoon now. Lights shone wanly from several of the buildings. The sun's last glow was softly fading in a cloudless sky. The world seemed to be holding its breath during the magical transition from day to night, from harsh reality to shadowed dreamtime.

Alfonso smiled. The time, the light, the sky were the most beautiful part of autumn. It reminded him of the start of the real new year, the beginning of school. Of the most pleasurable time of his life before the real world started to fuck him over.

What wonderful, crazy days those had been at the university in California. He had come fresh out of the army, too late for the fighting in Korea, too early for the madness in Vietnam, just in time for the campus uproars of the early 1960s. Oh, that had been a time. The civil rights movement had been his battlefield, his crusade, the crusade of his life. Never had he been so fulfilled. He had stood for something. Something big. He had been a spear-carrier in the army changing the world.

Ahead was the history building, though he was not certain if Enrique Armijo would be in his office. It was late for privileged history professors to be hanging around campus. Of the old gang only he and Armijo had returned home to stay. Alfonso to finish the extra year for his teaching credential and Enrique to get his Ph.D. All the others had come and gone. To California, Arizona, Michigan, New York, everywhere. It was not like the old days in Alfonso's father's time. Hardly anyone ever left home then. The few who went away to school always returned. This was their place. Their sanctuary. Their homeland.

A few young men and women loitered at the entrance to the history building, laughing flirtatiously. He sniffed the air, searching for the magical perfume of lust as he heard their unconsciously provocative banter.

As Alfonso entered the brightly lit hall he suddenly became aware of himself in a place he did not belong. He made a quick pass at his necktie to make certain that it was in place. He looked around nervously, ready to react to any challenge to his presence.

The door to Professor Armijo's office was ajar. A thin shaft of light streamed into the hall. Alfonso heard the sound of a man's voice. He pushed the door cautiously. Behind the desk talking on the telephone was his old schoolmate.

Enrique's face lit up in surprise. He motioned to come in, covering the mouthpiece. "Momentito," he said in a low voice. Then he continued on the telephone. Yes, yes. He had already made his travel reservations. No way would he miss the conference. Momentous things were afoot. His presentation would show them a thing or two. It would be good to blah, blah, blah again. Armijo made a face as he said this, and Alfonso smiled.

Books were crammed irregularly in the bookcase against the wall. Piles of periodicals overflowed the side table. Stacks of papers covered the desk. The left wall was covered with a print of an ancient map of the New World with legends written in Latin; it showed the reach of the Holy Roman Church toward ancient, Godforsaken lands that were fertile with pagan souls. A sign of one of the white man's worst diseases: missionizing.

Alfonso shook his head, thankful that ill-tempered fate had saved him from academia. Though at the time of his dismissal it was as if the earth had split, separating him from the good life forever.

The telephone receiver clanged noisily onto its base. "How's the Graffiti Kid? I saw your mural at the Southside Community Center. Worthy of a Picasso. Of a Rivera. Of a Gulley Jimson. I haven't seen you for ages. How the hell are you, mano?" Mano was short for hermano, which meant brother.

Same old bullshit, Alfonso thought. "If you weren't so busy promoting another trip to New York or wherever, you'd know what was going on around here."

Armijo's mobile face flashed a look of mock innocence. How can you say that of poor me? "So how the hell are you, mano? What you up to these days?"

"I'm on a crusade."

Armijo threw his hands out, palms up, and rolled his eyes. "Now what?"

"Justice."

"Ah. Well. No one ever went after that one before."

"Equality."

"I suppose you want liberty too. The whole enchilada."

"You son-of-a-bitch. You're the same smartass as always."

"If there's one thing teaching has taught me: go for the grants, stay in the best hotels at conferences, watch out for spinster professors who want to discuss their latest paper over cocktails. And even more so, beware of female graduate students bearing homemade tortillas; they'll want an A for C minus work. Not to speak of other complications."

Alfonso forced himself to smile. He should be used to Armijo's banter. He had known the man for twenty-five years. But he sensed something different about it today. It was like a hand gently extended to keep him away. As if Armijo was leery of what Alfonso might want of him. As if he had already made up his mind even before the question had been asked.

"You're looking well," Alfonso said, falling into banalities. "And your family?"

"I hear your mother died," Armijo said. "Qué lástima. How sad." Alfonso winced. He had not expected that sudden turn. For one of the few times in his life he was speechless. "You were always so close to her," Armijo said. "I always envied the relationship you had with your mother. It must have been a tremendous loss."

"It happens to us all. We must be thankful for what we have when we have it."

Armijo looked up solemnly and waved toward a chair. He seemed to be lost in thought, perhaps of his own mother who, Alfonso knew, had died when Enrique was a small boy. Now history was his mother and teaching was the umbilical cord that tied him to his heritage.

"Well, mano. What brings you here?" Spoken like a man used to being asked for favors.

"Like I said, I'm on a crusade."

Armijo's smile was almost wistful. "You don't still dream that the government will give us back the West? Return Aztlán to the people from whom the United States stole it?"

Alfonso shook his head. "Those sanctuary people. The ones who were arrested for saving refugees from El Salvador. Their lawyer is my cousin. Actually my first cousin's daughter."

"Ah. ¡Qué chingadera! When Uncle Sam wants to screw you over, he does it with all the grace of a mastodon in a tutu squashing a mosquito. She'll have her hands full with that one."

"Then you'll join me?"

"Join you? Join you for what?" There was alarm and suspicion in Armijo's voice.

"I'm organizing a march on the federal courthouse. We'll—"

"Wait a minute. Wait a minute. What do you mean *we,* paleface? What's all this march? What march? Is this another of your fire-bombing expeditions? Include me out."

Alfonso felt as if he would explode. Wouldn't anyone ever forget? Didn't anyone remember that he had never done such a thing? That what he had done was merely to say that the school administration would sure as hell have listened to their demands if someone had thrown a Molotov cocktail into the administration building? Unfortunately he had said it while leading a crowd of picketers. Said it into a bullhorn. With television cameras grinding and boom microphones picking up his every whisper. Only sure as hell he hadn't been whispering.

"That was a long time ago," Alfonso said. "I never set fire to anything except the school administration's fears. They never accused me of throwing a bomb. Inciting a riot was what they charged me with."

"And fired you."

"Best damn thing that ever happened to me. It freed me to become an artist. None of that bullshit, paranoid academia crap. Jesus! I still can't believe it."

"So what's this march?"

"To let the Feds know that they can't do this to us. To let them know that public opinion demands justice."

Armijo stared at him silently. Alfonso felt a chill. He saw his old friend—friend?—his onetime friend, through a lens of detachment. Look at that expensive necktie, he thought, wondering how askew his own knotted rag was. And the suit coat on the coat rack, one hundred percent wool. The shirt one hundred percent cotton set off by silver cufflinks. What had happened to the revolutionary of student days? He had turned into a bourgeois Chicano. A vendido, a sellout. Traded in his conscience for tenure. Worried about what people would think. Exhausted his manhood trying to make full professor. Suffering a convenient lapse of memory for all the pledges the Movimiento had made to preserve and advance la raza.

Armijo shook his head sadly. "All marching does is wear out shoe leather and mobilize the police. We don't have to do that anymore. We can take it to the courts. There are laws. There are other ways to get things done."

Didn't he see the absurdity of that? Alfonso thought. Take *what* to the courts? To the courts? The courts were trying these innocent people. How the hell were you going to take it to the courts when the courts were taking it to you?

"Whatever happened to your spirit?" Alfonso said, his voice rising. "Whatever happened to your sense of justice? Whatever happened to the Movimiento? Man, there used to be thousands of us fighting for all that was worth fighting for! Isn't there anyone left?" His voice trailed off into a confused plea, looking for confirmation of all the dreams about which he felt so passionately.

"It changed," Armijo said. "It grew up. It became institutionalized. There's César Chávez's farm workers. There are the politicos with their voter registration drives running for office. There are the legal defense people. The educators. Hell, Fonso. We teachers are on the forefront. I mean, when our own raza dropout rate guarantees that we remain the illiterate race forever, what more challenging crusade is there than education? Then, those of us who aren't on the front lines donate money. I mean, how can crusaders do their work when the bank account says overdrawn?"

"Fuck the bank account! What we need is a good blood-letting. Then they'll know we mean business. Then they'll know that something damn well better be done for the poor. Jesus, man. What happened to you? You used to be right up there storming the barricades with the best of us."

All the while Armijo was shaking his head. "The United States will never give back the Southwest they stole from Mexico to the descendants of those Mexicans. To us. Socialism will never work except in heaven—maybe. The way to power is through the vote. The way to the vote has to be paved by education. What the hell do you think I'm doing here on campus? I'm fighting the new revolution. The only one that will succeed."

It was Alfonso's turn to shake his head. Jesus. Give a man a steady paycheck and a full belly and suddenly he's a capitalist. Let a man become part of an institution, any institution, and he inherits the self-interest of the status quo. How was the world going to change when greed was in the saddle, riding the ignorant donkey of capitalism down the road to special privilege?

I never believed it would come to this, Alfonso thought. In the old days Armijo would have been more militant than me. Were they all like that now? All of the fire-eaters who wanted to change the world?

Alfonso glared at Armijo, saw the fatuous smile that wanted to please, that wanted him to understand. Understand what? That he had sold out? Yet, for all his disappointment, for all his anger, Alfonso did not feel the urge to attack that he might have at other times.

"Tell me," Alfonso said. "Who's still around? Is there anybody doing anything these days? How about Carrillo?"

"He's a lobbyist in California. Claims to have the state legislature in his hip pocket." Armijo rubbed his thumb and forefinger together to indicate how.

"And Panchito? Whatever happened to Panchito?"

"He married a rich Anglo and moved to New York."

"Or Jesús, for Christ's sakes. Whatever happened to Jesús?"

"Jesse's up in Colorado teaching English and writing the great Chicano novel."

Aw, shit! Alfonso thought. What am I doing wasting my time here? What the hell did I think I was going to find? A compadre?

He stood abruptly. "Hey, I gotta go, man. Just dropped by to say hello. To invite you to a great adventure. If you want to join us when we march on the feds, you know where to find me. I'll have a thousand of them out there. Just you wait and see."

To Alfonso's surprise, Armijo reached for his wallet. "I'd like to contribute to the cause," he said, holding out a bill. "That's the least I can do."

Alfonso was torn. He stared at the wrinkled green bill, then looked up, suppressing his anger. "I don't need any handouts. I have more important things to worry about."

He stood there, ready to hurry away before he smashed that bourgeois vendido in the face. Goddamn it, he thought, tears of rage welling up, insulted by Armijo's offer of money.

"It's sad, mano," Alfonso said, trying to restrain his anger, trying to make it sound like a joke. "You've become bourgeois. A goddamned bourgeois Chicano. Isn't that a laugh! What the fuck is a bourgeois Chicano anyway? Some kind of sick mutant. A traitor to his class."

Then he stormed out, slamming the door behind him.

❋ ❋ ❋

Alfonso was exhilarated as he marched, carrying his picket sign high. When he tired of walking he would stand on the corner, grasp the end of the handle to which the sign was nailed, and slowly wave it at approaching traffic. At times he would shout the words of another sign: "Down with U.S. gunboat diplomacy!"

When relatives, friends, or acquaintances walked by, he would shout their names and point to his sign. Some looked away with stony expressions and increased their pace. Alfonso's son, whom he had not seen in weeks, waved and shouted, "Atta boy, Pop!" Most would give a quick, curt nod and continue on their way. Occasionally someone would stop and talk and these he would attempt to press into service.

"Tomorrow," Peña would say. "By nine o'clock. I'll paint you the most magnífico sign you ever saw. Man, you'll be a walking work of art."

A boyhood friend who stopped shook his head and smiled. "Ay!" he said. "Don Quixote de los Frijoles."

As long as Alfonso and the people he invited were picketing alone, it was a great adventure. Then one day these others came, people he did not know, with their signs scrawled by a colorblind painter with palsy. All at once Peña's small band of crusaders was overwhelmed by a dozen strangers.

He was tempted to shout, "Hey! This is our corner. Find your own spot." But there were too many of them to risk starting a fight. With Alfonso's luck the cops would probably grab him, bloodied and beaten by superior forces, and haul him off to jail while the others went scot-free. He decided the two groups could coexist like small children in a sandbox playing alone side by side.

Most of the newcomers seemed all right. They generously shared their thermos bottles of coffee. While they didn't joke and laugh—they were a deadly serious group—they were pleasant enough and had an intensity that Alfonso shared. There were a few, however, who made him uncomfortable. Something about them struck him as false. They were *too* serious, *too* intense, *too* energetic, *too* helpful. As if they were trying to prove something.

Alfonso watched these few furtively, offering excuses when invited to attend one of their meetings. He remembered a recent newspaper article about a Chicago judge reprimanding the FBI for spying on legitimate groups opposed to U.S. policy in Central America. There was something about these few picketers that made him think of the FBI. And this was New Mexico, not Chicago. Who knew what a local judge might do? Peña was skitterish when it came to police, federal or otherwise. He had no desire to spend any more time in jail.

Each morning he waited for the chief defense attorney, his cousin Irene. On the days she came to court he waved, but she was too preoccupied to acknowledge his greeting. He could tell, though, that she was aware of him and that she appreciated his support. He only wished that he could do more to help, that he truly could have rallied a thousand supporters. He hoped that she had not taken his claim literally. The number had leaped to his tongue from his passionate desire to help and his anger at the way the so-called system screwed people over. He ardently wished that he could rally a thousand people—ten thousand.

One morning Alfonso's parish priest approached. He turned away, guilty at not having attended mass for weeks and not having made his confession since last Easter. When he turned back to see if the priest had gone, Father Gutiérrez was standing a few feet from him, waiting.

"That's a beautiful sign, Alfonso. I can see your artistic hand."

"Thank you, Father."

"I just wanted to tell you how much I'm looking forward to having dinner with you and Dolores tonight."

Dinner tonight? What the hell was this all about? Did Dolores really invite the priest or did that busybody invite himself in order to find out why Alfonso hadn't been to mass in so long?

"Our pleasure." His voice sounded anything but pleased.

Father Gutiérrez studied the other picketers. There was a judgmental frown on his face that Alfonso knew was more for him than for the others.

Tomás Gutiérrez was one of those old-fashioned priests who posted the names of parishioners who were behind in their collection pledges on the church bulletin board. Only the bulletin board was barely large enough; nearly half the parish was in arrears. His views on religion and politics were just to the right of Torquemada's, and Alfonso could imagine him condemning the sanctuary workers from the pulpit. Another good reason to miss mass.

"If only they would spend as much time in God's house as they do on the streets," the priest grumbled. "Then everything would be all right."

"Until dinner then, Father." Alfonso's words were a gentle shove to send the priest on his way.

Father Gutiérrez lifted his arms to the side and let them fall in resignation. "Ah, well," he said. "Until dinner, then."

* * *

Dinner went better than Alfonso had expected. It was a testament to the miraculous kitchen powers of his wife. She had conjured a meal worthy of a gourmet from nearly bare cupboards. A little this, a little that, something she had canned last winter, and whatever she had been able to borrow from neighbors. Plus, Alfonso suspected, what she had bought from the supermercado with the few pesitos she had probably squirreled away from his last unemployment check.

Dolores had been in a fluster when he came home, and she chased him out of the kitchen. Almost immediately Father Gutiérrez arrived so Alfonso did not have a chance to ask his wife what it was all about. She evaded him, too, by talking loudly from the kitchen to their guest as he sat in the front room. "Company," she hissed when Alfonso approached her. "Go stay with our company."

Now dinner was over. Father Gutiérrez, who had all but licked his plate, slid the chair back from the kitchen table and patted his tight, round stomach with a profusion of sighs. He put out his hand and shook his head to refuse another cup of coffee.

Now it comes, Alfonso thought. They've softened me up with food and polite conversation. It could only be one of two things. Either the priest is going to tell me to look harder for work, or he's going to demand that I stop parading in front of the courthouse. Maybe both. Stop protesting and go out and earn a living for your wife!

They moved to the front room where Alfonso offered the priest the good overstuffed chair. He and Dolores circled the sofa like cats searching for resting places, finally settling onto the cushions that had not completely collapsed.

Father Gutiérrez folded his hands across his stomach and sighed. "I have heard," he said, "that things have not been going too well for you lately, Alfonso."

Alfonso stared glumly at the priest, not uttering a sound, wondering if his wife had told him that, waiting for whatever was to follow. Dolores sat silently beside him.

"It was suggested that I come talk to you. I haven't seen you in church for some time." Alfonso turned toward Dolores, struggling to restrain his anger.

"You should not let pride blind you to the fact that we live in community," the priest continued. "We are here to help each other. Our parish reaches out to help those who are in temporary need. That's why I asked Dolores if I could pay a call."

So, Alfonso thought. The old busybody invited himself over. But who dared suggest that Father Gutiérrez come talk to him in the first place? Could it have been a neighbor? His old Chevy had died in the front yard two months ago, and anyone who wasn't blind could see him walking to the bus stop in the morning.

"I don't need any help," Alfonso said testily. "I've always been able to provide for my family."

"There are crises of the flesh as well as of the spirit," Father Gutiérrez said. "There are times when all of us need a helping hand. I understand that you are about to be evicted from your house."

Alfonso shot to his feet, his face red with anger. "Who told you that? Who told you that? It's a goddamned lie!" He looked wildly at Dolores, whose mouth had fallen open in shock.

It was then, almost as if on cue, that the slamming of car doors responded to the outburst of words. Through the window Alfonso saw his brother, his brother's wife, his sister, and her husband approach.

"Did you do this?" he shouted at Dolores. "Did you ask those bloodsucking cabrones to my house without my permission?"

Before Dolores could answer, there was a knock at the front door. The three of them sat frozen as the sound echoed through the silence. Then the priest rose, cautioning Alfonso with a stay of the hand, and opened the door.

"I won't talk to them," Alfonso shouted. "They'll have to talk to my lawyer."

"You can't afford a lawyer," his brother Cipriano said. "Let's get down to reality, man."

"Please, please," Father Gutiérrez said. "Let's not fight. We're here to reason together." He ushered in the newcomers who had stood hesitantly at the entrance to the room. "Please," he said, "come in. Get the chairs from the kitchen."

Father Gutiérrez put a hand on Alfonso's upper arm as reassurance and a gentle restraint. They formed a circle in the small living room, Alfonso, Dolores, and the priest where they had sat before, the others on the turquoise painted wooden chairs.

"First let's have a moment of silent prayer," the priest said. "Let's calm our hearts so we can reason together."

Alfonso sat open-eyed, breathing heavily, as the others closed their eyes. He was looking daggers at his brother, still smarting from the remark about not being able to afford a lawyer. Son-of-a-bitch, he thought. What does he know?

"Amen," Father Gutiérrez said. He smiled as if now everything was going to be all right. "I thought that it was time for a family council," he said. "I have known your family since your father inherited this house from your grandfather, who built it with his own hands. Sunday after Sunday I've watched you from the pulpit growing from children to adults and then becoming parents yourselves. Only a year ago I gave the last rites to your blessed mother who is in heaven now, anguishing over the bad blood between her children.

"So when Margarita came to talk to me," he nodded toward Alfonso's sister, "I thought it was time that we talked together. I apologize for not telling you, Alfonso. But if I had told you, you might not have come."

"You're damn right," Alfonso said.

"If you were really looking for work instead of making a public spectacle of yourself at the courthouse, you wouldn't be in this fix," Cipriano said.

"Please, please," Father Gutiérrez said.

"Trying to evict me from my mother's house," Alfonso said. "Without even a warning."

"Please."

"You're almost a year behind in the rent," Margarita said. "And Mother gave the house to us," meaning her and Cipriano.

"It was a mistake. She was unduly influenced when she was too sick to know what she was doing."

"Please! This bickering will get us nowhere," Father Gutiérrez said. "Instead of fighting we should be praying for the good Lord to help us see the way.

"Alfonso, whatever your feelings, whatever your mother's intentions, the house legally belongs to Margarita and Cipriano. The will has gone through the courts. Out of the kindness of their hearts they have allowed you to live here ever since your mother's death. They have every right to receive rent from the property they own."

Capitalist pigs! Alfonso thought. "I don't have a job. How can I pay rent when I don't have a job?"

"I've spoken to Dolores about helping at the rectory. Our housekeeper is retiring and—"

"Oh, no! Not my wife. What kind of a man do you think I am?"

"Fonso, it would only be part-time," Dolores pleaded. "It wouldn't get in the way of anything here at home."

"Fonso," Margarita said, "you're your own worst enemy."

"Well, if not your wife, what about you?" Cipriano said.

"I've got a job," Alfonso said. It was only a small lie. "At least until something better comes along. I'm going to be the newspaper's official artist for the sanctuary trial."

"You can't draw when you're picketing on the streets," Cipriano said.

Alfonso looked desperately around the room. The exits were blocked by his accusers, sitting in smug judgment as they confronted him. Their eyes burned with pleasure like cats contemplating a mouse before they killed and ate it.

"He's fighting for our rights," Dolores said. "Somebody has to stand up for our rights."

"How about your right to eat?" Margarita said.

"Or my right to collect rent?" Cipriano said.

"There are some things more important than rent or food," Dolores said. "There's justice and freedom."

"My God!" Cipriano said. "He's got you brainwashed. Those are his excuses so he can go on with his craziness instead of taking care of his family. Dolores, don't you get tired of living hand to mouth? Don't you want him to do his duty like every husband should?"

"It's his life," she said. "I agreed to it when I married him."

The priest, meanwhile, was shaking his head sadly. "Please," he said, "this is going nowhere. Let's start over from the beginning."

Alfonso suffered a growing frustration that started in his breast as a pinpoint of white heat and slowly spread until it was as if he was being consumed by the fires of hell. Even his wife's loyalty did not cool him. He was too distraught to lash out so he sat there, impotent, seeing the others through a red haze, hearing their distorted voices as if through a ghostly filter.

Above, away from the house as he longed to be, he imagined his mother in the clear blue sky, seated on a celestial throne, weeping as she looked down on them.

"First let's talk about the house. Margarita, Cipriano, you don't want to throw your brother and his wife out in the street."

There was no response.

Father Gutiérrez tried another tack. "If this house had been willed to all three of you, that would have been worth so much to each."

"But it wasn't, Father," Cipriano said. "It was left to just the two of us."

The priest put out a hand for silence. "Just consider if it had," he continued. "That might have paid for a certain number of years of rent."

"But it wasn't, Father," Margarita said.

"Look, Father," Cipriano said. "The house is worth so much a month rent. Even if all three of us owned it—which is not so—each of us would be entitled to one-third of the rent. Isn't that true? Well, Margarita and I have never received what we're entitled to even if Alfonso owned part of the house."

"I'll go to work," Dolores said. "Fonso will too. It's just that jobs for artists are hard to find. Not everyone appreciates true talent. Isn't that right, Fonso?"

"What's needed is a little more compassion," Father Gutiérrez said. "Here's your brother, your own blood, left out of your mother's will for whatever reason. He is in need, deeply in need. You may not feel that you have to give him a share of the house, but perhaps you could find it in your hearts to forgive him what rent he owes. After all, what's past is past. As for the future, Dolores is willing to work. We have a place for her in the rectory. And Alfonso is working for the newspaper."

The words flowed back and forth over Alfonso like the ebb and flow of the ocean. He heard snatches of conversation here and there: the crash of a wave, the washing of a foamy sheet of water as it slowed until it was absorbed by the sandy shore.

His life was being decided for him, and yet he could not rouse himself enough to protest.

In a way it was a relief for things to be decided by others. The old priest was being helpful instead of scolding him. Even the thought of Dolores going to work did not pain him so much now. His pride was dissolving the way the ocean of words was sinking into oblivion, leaving him with a feeling of relief, and he had a vision of his mother on her celestial throne smiling down on him.

The red haze faded so that he could see his brother and sister across the room listening earnestly to Father Gutiérrez. The fires of hell receded until there was only that pinpoint of heat in his breast. It remained there, a scar from the ordeal. Yet deep inside, there was an uncomfortable feeling that the pinpoint would have to be acknowledged. That there was something yet to be done to relieve him of his lifelong anguish and frustration.

"Then it's settled," he heard Father Gutiérrez say. "Alfonso, I want to see you at mass next Sunday."

It was all Alfonso could do to feebly nod his head.

* * *

Alfonso scurried through the courtroom door for a seat on the aisle so that he could have elbow room while he sketched. Prospective jurors filed in, overflowing the spectators' seats. They would be selecting the jury today.

He surveyed the stage of the courtroom: the judge's bench, the witness stand, the podium where the attorneys would stand to question the witnesses, all with chrome microphones shiny like burnished silver. On one wall hung both sides of the great seal of the United States: one with the eagle, the other with the pyramid, giant replicas of what appeared on the back of a one-dollar bill. On each was engraved "United States District Court. New Mexico." The U.S. flag hung alongside the bench. On the opposite wall from the jury box was a bookcase with its leather-bound contents. In front of the bench were the tables where the opposing lawyers and the defendants were gathering. A railing separated the business of the court from the spectators.

Something was missing, Alfonso thought. Color. Where was the color in this scene? Yes. There was the red, white, and blue of the flag, hanging in folds from its pole. The bronze seals on the side wall. The wine-colored books. The brown of polished wood: the bench, the witness stand, the jury box, the railing—the boring sameness that overwhelmed the court-room with its bland face of neutrality.

Maybe the actors, Alfonso thought, though few of the prin-cipals had yet made their appearance. The court clerk checked what looked like a small, enclosed Ferris wheel—the box from which slips with jurors' names would be withdrawn. She was wearing black pants and a print blouse with pink tropical flow-ers on a black background. The lawyer sorting through a folder at the prosecution's table was in a navy blue suit with white shirt, red and blue striped tie, and black slip-on shoes with leather tassels. Maybe under that boring facade he wore bikini shorts with red hearts on them, Alfonso thought. At least the older woman at the defense's table was worthy of an artist's sketch, with bright red suit, white sweater over a white open-neck shirt, set off by stylishly coiffed silver hair.

Well, this wasn't a fashion show or a convention of artists' models. Even if a newspaper or magazine was interested in buying his sketches, they'd probably print them in black and white.

In truth, he didn't have much hope of selling his work. He was here strictly to please his wife and to show good faith to his brother and sister and Father Gutiérrez.

But it was good to get back to what he did best. From an artistic point of view it was better than painting picket signs. He could always march before and after the proceedings.

He carefully surveyed the empty stage and took a pencil from his pocket. There, he thought. That's an interesting line, with that nice shadow falling across the jury box.

He lost himself in a sketch as the rest of the principal play-ers drifted onstage. He awoke with a start when the court was asked to rise. That's a face for you, he thought, staring at the tiny, gray-haired judge who entered. A regular Chihuahua who cried out to be caricatured.

Then he became aware of others across the railing. His cousin in a tailored turquoise suit and white blouse, set off by a necklace of silver rain and turquoise earrings. Dark, dark eyes set deep in bronzed skin—a true daughter of the Southwest. Another of the defense attorneys, a man, wore the uniform of his profession: the navy blue suit, white shirt, and boring necktie out of the same mold as the other male lawyers.

Alfonso was looking them over carefully, studying them for those expressions and gestures that brought out their indi-viduality. The diminutive Chihuahua intensity of the judge. The repressed tension of Stanley Miller, the U.S. Attorney, with his superficial aura of calm that Alfonso sensed was not his true nature. Then his cousin: brisk, businesslike, definitely in charge like some of the queen bees in his family.

He was putting the finishing touches on a sketch when the judge swore in the prospective jurors. Then the court clerk began to draw out and read names from the small Ferris wheel. The first fourteen people exchanged seats with those already in the jury box while the others sat in rows of spectator seats in the order that their names were drawn.

Alfonso was busy sketching when the judge explained the selection process, followed by a reading of the indictment. He was looking for interesting faces in the jury panel.

The judge began his questions, asking for a show of hands for affirmative answers, like being in school again. "Are any of the prospective jurors acquainted with the lawyers of the defendants in this case?" No one raised a hand.

Then other relevant questions. "Have any of you ever served on a jury involving charges similar to those in this case?" Several hands went up, and Alfonso focused on a woman in her early forties with a distinctive white streak of hair that rose from her widow's peak like a skunk's stripe.

The bailiff carried a portable microphone to each of the panelists as their names were called out by the judge. Alfonso kept busy sketching, hardly hearing the answers until they got to his model, Ramona López.

"Mrs. López," the judge said. "What was the nature of the case?"

"Drugs, your honor." In addition to the indictment of alien smuggling, one of the defendants was arrested with marijuana in his possession.

"Would you explain, please."

"A man accused of selling drugs."

"What was the outcome of the case?"

"He was guilty as sin."

"If you are selected for the jury, could you base your decision on the facts of this case and this case alone?'

"Yes, sir."

Then on to more questions to the entire group. "Have any of you ever appeared in court as a defendant to a felony?' One hand rose tentatively. "Mrs. Johnson."

Her voice was barely audible, "A speeding ticket."

"Speeding tickets don't count, Mrs. Johnson." The woman, looking confused, glanced nervously away from the judge.

"Do any of you feel that testimony of a law enforcement officer must automatically be believed?" No hands.

"Do any of you or your immediate family work for a law enforcement agency?"

This time several hands came up, and the judge asked each in turn whether or not the testimony of law enforcement officers must automatically be believed. All agreed that even law enforcement officers can make mistakes.

"Is there anyone who believes that a person's profession automatically exempts him or her from the possibility of committing a crime? For example, a member of the clergy, a law enforcement officer, a judge." A wave of suppressed laughter swept through the panel but again no hands.

"Has anyone in your family or anyone you know been involved with controlled substances, that is drugs, in any way? I know this is a sensitive subject, but I must ask the question. Please be completely honest. If you prefer, you can approach the bench with your answer."

A number of hands went up. "Mr. Lawrence Walker," the judge said, calling the first person, "you may approach the bench."

Alfonso watched the short, stocky older man walk forward with a slight limp. His bearing was rigid and military. His gray hair was cut short, standing stiffly at attention. Would he make an interesting sketch? he thought. No. Too uptight.

Others followed, talking in low voices to the judge while surrounded by the two attorneys and the court reporter who recorded their conversations.

Then more questions, boring questions that Alfonso totally ignored. At last the final two questions: "Is there anything so abhorrent about the charges in this case that would prevent you from serving on the jury?" No hands.

"Is there anything at all about this case that would prevent you from rendering a verdict based on the facts entered as evidence?" For the last time, no hands.

The morning had moved fairly quickly. Alfonso looked at the few ideas that he had sketched, still not taken with any of them. He looked toward the prospective jurors, wondering what they were really like beneath the surface of their answers. Would the defendants really get a fair trial? Did the panelists answer truthfully? No one liked to admit in public that they were prejudiced, that they had already made up their minds, that they really believed that if someone was tried in court they were automatically guilty. They could have answered every question properly and truly believed their answers. But somehow, deep down, beneath logic and thought there could be prejudices so ingrained that they weren't even aware of them. *The defendants wouldn't be here if they weren't guilty. Convict the bastards!*

The court adjourned for lunch. After lunch the two attorneys would have their turns questioning the members of the panel.

* * *

How long had this damned thing been going on? Alfonso wondered. Whatever, he was bored—had been bored for days with all of the talk, talk, talk. He had sketched everybody that was of any importance—not once, but two, three times. The officers of the court may have looked different, had different last names, but they were brothers under the skin. Exchangeable cogs in the reactionary chain that was choking justice to death. Jesus, you would at least have expected a little more understanding, a little more sympathy from a judge named Jaramillo.

Then, of course, he had only sold three of his sketches. He couldn't believe how cheap these newspaper editors were. It worked out to a few centavitos an hour. Jesus! Give me bread and water instead.

He sat looking intently at prosecuting attorney Miller. He knew the type. Tall, rugged looking son-of-a-bitch with his soft drawl of a voice, trying to disguise his true identity as a storm trooper. Peña squinted, letting his imagination clothe the prosecuting attorney in the proper uniform. Not the expensive navy blue suit with all the affluent middle-class paraphernalia—but in brown shirt and hobnail stomping boots, a visored hat emblazoned with a swastika like one on the arm band of the shirt. Heil! He sketched quickly, coming alive for the first time during today's tedium. Alfonso surveyed the finished sketch with satisfaction. Gotcha! he thought, addressing the prosecuting attorney.

Then he looked at the judge. This would be easy. A Chihuahua in a flowing black robe, a giant gavel in his hand raised to smash a statue of blindfolded Justice, a cartoonist's balloon out of his mouth with super-size lettering to signify a loud bark from a small dog: *"Objection overruled!"*

Alfonso smiled and looked at the man in the witness box that the prosecuting attorney was questioning for the second time. He started to sketch García's head on a round cockroach body, a thin buglike leg holding a roach clip with a giant, dark colored cigarette whose smoke clouded the upper part of the drawing. But no. He drew a giant X through it and flipped the page. No. It wasn't fair. The witness was a refugee, a man who had suffered and who was suffering once again in this police state atmosphere. They were going to nail him for possession once the trial was over. He was lucky they hadn't caught him in Texas. Those Tejanos would have locked him up and thrown away the key. All for a piddling bag of Mary Jane.

What else? he thought. He could draw García as a mojado, a wetback. But the man wasn't Mexican, and it wasn't funny. Besides, García crossed the Río Grande in a van, not wading through the water.

No. García was a victim. Another of the poor and power-less. How could you do a caricature of a victim? Only the devil would let an artist be so cruel. No. If he drew García it would have to be as a man crucified. The cruel nails of politics and law spiked through his bleeding hands. His eyes uplifted, straining to see through the dark cloud that blocked the sun of compassion.

The sound of the gavel broke his spell. Startled, he jumped to his feet and his tablet slid off his lap onto the floor. He quickly stooped to retrieve it before he was shoved into the aisle and out of the courtroom.

One o'clock. Free until one o'clock. He ambled out, wondering what he would do for the next two hours. Make another trip to the newspaper, he decided. To see what he could sell.

✳ ✳ ✳

Alfonso entered the courtroom early so he could get his favorite seat on the aisle. He was relieved to be off his feet, having spent part of his lunch hour parading in front of the building. The picketers had dwindled to a hardcore few, so he felt obligated to join them when he could.

It was the defense's turn now. While he was interested in his cousin's performance, the incessant talk still bored him. Alfonso had already decided that the defendants would be found guilty. The court system was a fix. You could tell by the way the judge favored the prosecution. Never mind the testimony. Never mind the truth. What did the law have to do with truth, anyway? It was a matter of rules, and whoever had the power made the rules. However bad. However unjust. However immoral.

He had lost his enthusiasm for sketching that had made the morning session tolerable. Who else could he caricature? Maybe a reporter—if he could recognize one. But what the hell good would that do? The damned editor at the Herald had told him that they didn't publish caricatures. The only underground newspaper in town didn't pay frijoles. Yet he felt a savage urge to sketch a journalist. He would look like a fox. With pointed nose sniffing the air for scandal, sly eyes of distrust, and an open jaw of pointed teeth slavering in anticipation.

Alfonso doodled, half listening to the testimony from the defense's first witness, another refugee. He lightly sketched two refugees, each on a cross with eyes uplifted. Christ and the two thieves. Who would be Christ? He had only drawn the two thieves. How about showing them stealing across the border? No, he thought as he crossed it out with bold, heavy strokes. It doesn't work.

Macario Zamora confirmed the morning witness's testimony. The two of them, Zamora and García, had met at a refugee camp near the Guatemalan border. Zamora had the money; García had youth and two good legs. They hitchhiked and rode buses north. They spent almost a month in Juárez,

Mexico, searching for someone trustworthy to guide them across the border.

They learned about Zorro from some men in a cantina. Yes, they had been warned about coyotes, smugglers. But they didn't see any other way, and Zamora's leg was not healing. Zamora paid half the money when they boarded the van in Juárez, promising the rest when they were safe in the United States. Once there, García promised to help him get to Santa Fe.

No, he knew nothing about marijuana. García had never mentioned it. He did not seem like the kind of person who went in for that sort of stuff.

On and on, Alfonso thought. Nothing new. He looked for something interesting about the witness to sketch. Nothing. How can you sketch a white-haired man with a limp without making it seem cruel? He wouldn't be able to sell it, anyway.

He started to think about his wife and his brother and sister. Dolores coming home from her half-day at the rectory, eager for his report. Sorry. No sale. His brother and sister knocking at the door the first of the month, palms outstretched. Dolores peeling the rumpled bills one by one from that pinched little purse. Alfonso could feel the shame already. His wife—the woman—earning the money and paying the rent. That was a man's job. A man's!

"Alberto Romero."

Another witness. More of the same. Only this man had crossed the border with his wife. No coyote. No priest. No underground railroad. Just walked across. Only those pigs from la migra had picked up his wife and shipped her back to El Salvador, back to her death.

How do you draw a man without a wife? he thought. Draw half a man. How do you draw a man who can't support his wife? Same thing. Bad idea.

The questioning was over. Both defense and prosecution had had their say. Another day in court. Now he would have to go home and face his own questioning. Sorry. No sale.

* * *

The next morning Alfonso sat glumly in the courtroom. It had not gone well last night. Not because of Dolores, God love her. But that damned Father Gutiérrez had dropped by to see how he was doing. Old busybody. What could Alfonso say? The nosy old cleric must have already grilled Dolores, who was not mean enough to tell him to mind his own business. She would be loyal and put a good face on things, but then Gutiérrez was shrewd enough to read between the lines.

Last night lingered as a burning in the pit of his stomach. Then that damned bailiff had blocked his way this morning, so that huge woman had taken his regular seat. He would have asked her to move except that he was too angry and wasn't sure if he could control himself. So he took the aisle seat in the row ahead, trembling with frustration.

Everything was filtered through the haze of last night. He felt the urge to shout at the judge. Or make an obscene gesture—the old middle finger. The prosecuting attorney looked like a gorilla. Even his cousin, his lovely cousin, seemed cold and hard today.

Then they brought in the next witness for the defense. An uninteresting, rawboned desert rat with pale eyes and streaked yellow hair that looked like tobacco stains on a heavy smoker's fingers. He was disguised in a business suit and tie but that didn't fool anybody.

"Your name please?" Irene Bustamante began.

"Martin Young."

"Your occupation?"

"I'm the chief administrator for the Emma Lazarus Committee in Washington, D.C."

"What is the Emma Lazarus Committee?"

"We're a citizens' watch committee, funded by donations, that works on behalf of people from other countries wanting to immigrate to the United States. We lobby Congress to enact legislation that lives up to the ideals of our Founding Fathers on issues affecting immigration. We monitor various government agencies—the State Department, the Justice Department—to make certain that laws are carried out fairly. We coordinate with organizations outside of this country, the United Nations for example, on behalf of people wanting to enter the United States."

Alfonso turned with sudden attention toward the witness. Here was something that spoke to him. "Give me your tired, your poor, your huddled masses yearning to breathe free."

"How long has the Committee been active?"

"For almost five years. I resigned from the U.S. State Department to help found it."

"You resigned?"

"Yes."

"Why is that?"

"I had some differences of opinion with the administration's policy on refugees from certain countries."

"Objection, your honor!"

It was as if Alfonso had been jabbed with a needle. He turned quickly toward the gorilla who had dared object. The prosecuting attorney was glaring angrily at Alfonso's cousin. His cousin! The burning in his stomach radiated out in a widening circle. Let her speak! he mumbled to himself. Let him answer!

"Will you approach the bench," the judge said to the two attorneys.

Alfonso could see the Chihuahua yapping at Bustamante. Then the gorilla was saying something, his angry face thrust at Irene, looming over her like King Kong ready to pounce. Then Irene came right back at them, not giving an inch. Then the Chihuahua again, brows furrowed. Top dog gets the last bark.

"Please rephrase the question," the judge said. He sounded not so much exasperated as—not bored—perhaps weary.

"You resigned from the U.S. State Department?"

"That's correct."

"Has the Emma Lazarus Committee been involved in the problems of refugees from—"

"Objection!"

"Counsel for the defense, please approach the bench."

Then the Chihuahua was yapping at her again, more intensely this time, warning her no doubt, and she was nodding her head. What kind of justice is this, Alfonso thought, when you can't even ask a question? The fix is on, he thought. This isn't a trial. And he started to feel the edges of his control slipping.

The defense attorney left the bench. Her expression was grim and her lips pressed tight in a hard line.

"Counsel for the defense," the judge said, more for the record that the court reporter was transcribing than for her, "you will please restrict the wording and subject of your questions as ruled upon. I don't want to warn you again. Now please rephrase the question."

"Mr. Young, has the Emma Lazarus Committee been involved in the problems of undocumented aliens from Central America?"

"Yes, we have."

"Would you describe the Committee's work?"

"Objection, your honor!"

"Objection sustained. Please strike that question from the record."

"Has the Emma Lazarus Committee cooperated with international organizations on the problems of undocumented aliens from Central America?"

"Yes, we have. The United Nations among them, plus a number of political allies in the United States."

"Would you describe—"

"Objection, your honor."

"Your honor," the defense attorney protested, "I haven't even finished asking the question."

"Objection sustained."

They're not going to let him testify, Alfonso thought. "Wrong!" he shouted without thinking.

Eyes turned in alarm toward Alfonso, tightly coiled, ready to explode. A buzz of voices swept through the courtroom. "Order!" the judge said, pounding his gavel.

Irene Bustamante turned, her gaze sweeping across the spectators, hesitating imperceptibly as her eyes met those of Alfonso Peña. She turned back to the witness.

"Mr. Young, I believe that you have with you some information from the State Department relevant to this trial."

"That's correct."

"What is the nature of this information?"

"It's a tape recording."

"Your honor, the defense would like permission to play the tape for the jury."

"Objection, your honor!"

"Will counsels please approach the bench."

Oh, God. What now? Alfonso thought. He looked up and saw the bailiff watching him. Maybe if I sketch something I'll calm down, he thought. The Statue of Liberty, and beside it a man in judge's robes and fire helmet gripping a hose from which he's aiming a torrent of water at the flaming torch. But his hands were trembling so that he couldn't do the drawing justice.

They were talking up there again. Arguing. Their mouths flapping, their faces in ever changing animation, their eyes grim. Back and forth. Like a three-player Ping-Pong game. Finally the lawyers returned to their places, and the judge looked out at the courtroom.

"The court will recess for twenty minutes," the judge said. "We'll reassemble at ten-forty." The two lawyers followed him into chambers, Irene carrying a tape cassette in her left hand.

Why the hell can't they let us all hear it? Alfonso thought.

His imagination followed them into chambers. What had they recorded? The most important testimony of all, he decided.

"Excuse me." The spectators moved along his row like parts on an assembly line, heading for the corridor and a smoke or for the rest rooms. "Excuse me."

Alfonso looked to the row behind, planning to reclaim his seat if the old cow had left. But she hadn't, still sitting immobile like a tree that had taken root.

What was on the tape? Alfonso wondered again. Something damning for the prosecution. Someone high up. In the State Department or Department of Justice. Or even in the executive branch. Someone spilling his guts about how they were going to screw the poor refugees because they didn't want to embarrass their allies who were in power. Maybe the President himself, saying we didn't want any more foreigners in this country. They take our jobs or live on welfare. Survive on a can of tomatoes a day. Then send their money back to the old country to support a bunch of brown-faced illegitimate children.

He looked at the clock, high above the entrance to the courtroom. Only five minutes had passed. Good God! Why was time moving so slowly?

Then he glanced at the people still in the courtroom, hoping to see someone worth drawing. But his hands were still trembling, and he gave up the idea even though there was a strange, ugly man sitting in the back row who was a subject worthy of a Goya.

He looked at the clock again, watching the second hand make its interminable round. Why is it, he thought, that the first of the month when bills are due comes around so fast, while twenty minutes can be an eternity?

Then he closed his eyes and tried to think good thoughts. About his wife Dolores, his most adoring fan, who thought that he could do no wrong. How he hated to disappoint her, even though she never said a word. Of his beautiful daughter in California with her engineer husband, making her way up in the world. Even his rascal of a son, smiling and waving as Alfonso walked the picket line. "Atta boy, Pop!"

Maybe he could say a little prayer. Not so much from piety as from superstition, though he had always gone to church when he thought about it. He silently mouthed the Lord's Prayer, whispering with special fervor those words about our daily bread. Oh, yes, he thought. Let's make sure You give us our daily bread. Today! Maybe I can sell another sketch if I could just find something worth drawing.

The spectators started to drift back in. Alfonso opened his eyes. When he turned, he saw that the large woman behind him had left. He reclaimed the seat quickly, settling into the warmth left by that huge bottom.

The court clerk stood and asked them to rise. It was like the curtain going up for the third act of a stage play, the actors frozen, waiting for the right moment to begin.

"Your honor," Irene Bustamante said, "since the tape recording has been ruled inadmissible, I have no more questions."

No more questions?

"Outrage!" Alfonso Peña jumped to his feet, shaking a fist. "Outrage! What kind of justice is this? It's a fix. A kangaroo court. A blasphemy on the—"

The courtroom exploded in an uproar. The bailiff rushed at Alfonso, who was now shouting obscenities. The judge pounded his gavel. "Order! Order!"

The bailiff and another uniformed man grabbed Alfonso, lifted him so that his feet barely touched the floor and rushed him out of the courtroom, as Peña looked back toward the judge, still shouting.

* * *

Maybe they had a right to remove him from the courtroom, he finally concluded. But they had no right to lock him up. He hadn't committed a crime. What was a little disagreement between adversaries in court? Wasn't that what trials were supposed to be about? Yet they had carried him off and thrown him in a holding cell. As a precaution, the bailiff said. They had seen him picketing the courthouse. They had been warned about an organized conspiracy to disrupt the trial.

They were afraid of him, Alfonso concluded, not without a touch of pride. Except that while he stewed in a cell he was unable to telephone his wife. When they finally allowed him a telephone call, he realized that their phone had been disconnected for nonpayment. His son was at work, and he didn't know the number. In desperation, hating the very idea of it, he telephoned his brother at his hair salon who finally agreed to notify Dolores.

The next morning, while the jury was still deliberating, he was called before Judge Jaramillo. The judge looked through his sketchbook, left behind when he had been rudely ejected from the courtroom. He paused at one sketch, then at another, no doubt drawings of the Chihuahua. The judge stared hard at the cowed but unrepentant Alfonso with a hangman's eye. He pounded his gavel and declared a stiff fine—or equivalent jail time. Bastard judge, Alfonso thought. No sense of humor.

It took Dolores the rest of the day to raise the money. Meanwhile back to a cell where Alfonso seethed at the injustice of it all. Thank God, before the afternoon was over he was free.

"Did you hear?" Dolores said. "The jury reached a verdict."

"How the hell could I hear when I was locked up?" Then, "Guilty!" he said. A foregone conclusion.

"No. No. They were let free."

Holy mother of God! Will miracles never cease? "Maybe I did some good after all," he said, still not believing what he had heard.

"Of course, Fonso. There's only one problem." Oh, Christ, he thought. What now? "The money." Meaning the money borrowed to pay the fine.

I'll have to find a job, he thought. I'll really have to do something, even if it's hiring myself out to dig ditches.

"Don't worry," he said. "Haven't I always taken care of you?" She was tactful enough—or perhaps loving enough—not to disagree.

THE DANCING SCHOOL

There are girlhood memories so vivid that you never forget them. Even now after more than thirty years I can see Annie Laurie Trujillo the day she came into our fourth grade class at the little country school in Los Rafas, New Mexico. It was late January. The new semester had started two weeks before. There was a thin scum of gray snow outside. Then in walked this girl wearing a winter coat that must have been tailored for a child millionaire. With a little fur collar and cuffs, and wool the color of camel's hair. It was as unlike the homemade coat I wore as diamonds from coal. Unlike any little girl's coat I had ever seen except in the movies.

"Who does she think she is?" my best friend, Sonia Gonzales, whispered. Meaning the movie star coat and the dress underneath. The dress was much cuter than our Sunday go-to-mass dresses. Anyway, most of the girls were wearing jeans.

What I had stared at even more than her clothes was her flaming red hair. It was an unbelievable color and naturally curly. Who could ever believe that color? Flaming red hair didn't go with brown skin and little country schools where kids spoke Spanish as much as they spoke English. Red hair went with pasty-white faces covered with freckles and snooty Anglo girls who lived in town.

"I bet it's a wig," Sonia whispered.

"Boys and girls," the teacher said. "This is Annie Laurie Trujillo." We couldn't help but titter. What a name! Then some boy in back started to hum the song "Annie Laurie," and the class went into hysterics.

"Students!" the teacher shouted. She always called us students when she was trying to get us to behave, exploding the word at us. "Students!" Banging on her desk with a pointer. "Annie Laurie just moved here from El Paso," she said, trying to distract us from laughing. "How many of you have ever been to El Paso, Texas?"

Not a hand went up. Maybe it was because most of us were still laughing and hadn't heard, but I don't think so. We seldom went into town which was less than five miles away. How would we ever travel 250 miles south to El Paso?

Annie Laurie wasn't fazed by the commotion. She didn't even blush, which would have been hard to see because her complexion was almost as dark as mine.

"Sit right here," the teacher said, leading her to the desk on my left. "Rebecca can help you with the arithmetic lesson." Then to the rest of the class, "Now students, back to work."

Annie Laurie stared into my eyes and flashed me a smile that said she wanted to be friends. I wasn't buying any. The only thing she had going for her was her naturally curly hair which drove me into a fit of jealousy. My mother never had time to do anything with my straight hair. Especially now that Papá had gone "to sing with the angels," as she put it. He had volunteered to be a soldier and had been killed in Korea the first month he was there. But I didn't talk about that. Not even to my best friend. It was a dark, secret lump in my chest that I didn't know what to do with. I was an oddity—the only one in class who didn't have a father.

The next day Miss Movie Star wore another show-off outfit which we heard before we saw. She came down the hall with the same dress and coat as the day before. But this noise accompanied her. "Ka—lak, ka—lak! Ka—lak, ka—lak. Ka—lak, ka—lak!"

Annie Laurie was wearing black patent leather shoes with taps. It didn't take long for the teacher to call her to the desk for a whispered talk. At lunch Annie Laurie went home and came back with regular thick-soled, scuffed shoes like the rest of us.

"Serves her right," Sonia said. "She's nothing but a fancy pants."

After that it was downhill for Annie Laurie. She wore the same coat, the same dress, the same shoes, and the same secret smile every day that week.

"She's a fake!" Sonia said at recess. "She's not rich at all. Besides, I saw her whirling around showing off. Her dress went up so high you could see everything." Then she began to sing:

"I saw London.

I saw France.

I saw ragged underpants."

And she gave me a wicked smirk.

Meanwhile, Annie Laurie was trying hard to be my pal. "You're the smartest girl in class," she said to me when we were doing arithmetic. "That makes you the leader."

Well, I didn't know about being the leader, although I did figure I was the smartest—boy or girl. I didn't need her to tell me that.

"Why don't you come to my house and play after school?" she said. "I'll let you wear my tap shoes."

"I'm busy," I said.

"What's your father like?" she asked the next day at recess.

I froze. How dare she ask a question like that? I was so angry I couldn't say a word, even if I'd wanted to.

Then she lowered her voice to a whisper, even though there was no one within twenty feet of us. "I don't have a father." She looked at me, waiting for a reaction.

"Everybody has a father," I finally said, feeling like I wanted-ed to scream out the words.

"Well I don't!" She was trying to intrigue me, but she didn't. What she did was make me look at her a little more kindly because we shared something, even though she didn't know it.

"So what?" I said.

"If you come to my house, I'll show you his picture."

Boy! I thought. How can you show a picture of a father that doesn't exist? But I was curious. "Maybe," I said. "If I can try on your tap shoes."

She did a funny little shuffle with her feet that ended with her arms outstretched, one foot in front of the other, and a bright, expectant smile like she was waiting for applause. "I'll meet you right here after school," she said. "Don't tell anyone." I ran off to join my friends who were yelling at me to hurry up.

Next day I walked home with Annie Laurie. The biggest house along the way was tall with a steep rather than a flat roof. The adobe bricks had been smoothed over with mud and then whitewashed so it didn't have the dirt look of all the others.

"Who lives there?" Annie Laurie asked. "They must be rich."

She asked me who lived in all the houses that we passed. The small, flat-roofed, dirt-colored ones too. She would stop and stare when I mentioned the name of one of the girls in our class, as if she was memorizing the house.

Her house was one of the poorest of a poor bunch. Far back from the main road, over the main irrigation ditch, tucked in the corner of a field as if it were an afterthought. Or maybe an old corral converted for poor relations who had nowhere else to go. It even had the faint aroma of corral, I thought. Goats.

"Annie Laurie, did you bring a friend?"

Her mother made an entrance, sweeping in like royalty entering the grand ballroom. She wore a dress that was the adult equivalent of the dress Annie Laurie wore to school. I was too intimidated to wonder if that was the only dress Mrs. Trujillo had.

"You must be Rebecca Montoya," she said, taking my hand and holding it in the two of hers as if—I don't know what. "You're the leader of the fourth grade class."

I shot Annie Laurie an eyeful of daggers, but she just smiled sweetly. "She wants to try on my tap shoes," Annie Laurie said.

"Oh," her mother said, "are you into the dance? How wonderful. See, Annie Laurie. I told you there'd be cultured people here."

Into the dance? I thought. What kind of talk was that? And as for culture, I wasn't sure what the word meant.

Annie Laurie ran into the other room of the two-room house and returned with the black patent leather shoes. I forgot about being "into the dance" and "culture." They were so pretty!

"Here. Put them on."

While I did that, Annie Laurie dragged out a small wooden platform to put in the center of the earthen floor. The floor was the old-fashioned kind that you sprinkled with water and packed down and left to dry. My grandmother's house used to have a dirt floor like that. Now everybody had wooden floors.

I stood on trembling legs like a newborn filly anxious to take her first steps. I felt myself transformed into an elegant lady. A princess wearing magic shoes. If this was culture, I was crazy about it.

"On the boards," Annie Laurie said. "That way you can really hear them."

"Ka—lak, ka—lak! Ka—lak, ka—lak! Klak, klak, klak, klak!"

I couldn't believe it. I was Shirley Temple dancing with Bojangles. I was a ballerina. I was an eagle, soaring above the earth. I just had to have shoes like this, no matter what. I'd give up Christmas and my birthday for a thousand years!

Mrs. Trujillo nodded as she watched me thrashing about in a noisy and uncoordinated way. I stopped after a few minutes, sweaty and out of breath.

"You have a natural gift," Mrs. Trujillo said. "Doesn't she, Annie Laurie?" Annie Laurie nodded cautiously. Mrs. Trujillo's eyes sparkled. "Do you think we should tell her?" she asked her daughter.

Annie Laurie looked at me solemnly, trying to make up her mind. I stood in the center of the wooden platform, feeling myself being judged. Hoping that I would be judged worthy. Of what, I wasn't sure. Whatever it was, I wanted Annie Laurie to say yes.

Finally, after eons, she nodded abruptly. Her mother turned toward me with a secretive air. She spoke softly, confidentially. "I'm going to start a dancing school, and you're the first to know."

My eyes widened, and my heart gave a loud thump. "Can I come?" I asked, my voice timid and hopeful.

Mother and daughter looked at each other in silence. "I should talk to your mother first," Mrs. Trujillo finally said.

"Oh, would you?" I pleaded.

Meanwhile, Annie Laurie came over and pressed the fronts of the tap shoes, searching for my toes. "What size do you wear?" she asked. Then to her mother, "She'll have to have shoes. And an outfit."

"Whoopee!" I shouted.

When my mother came home from work, I told her about the dancing school. Since Mother was a big, friendly woman, she didn't wait for Annie Laurie's mother to come over. She went to their house right after dinner, leaving me to do the dishes and my homework.

When Mother came back she was actually gushing. You'd have thought the whole thing was her idea. We girls would have all the advantages of town girls. No more of this dumb farmer, country hick stuff. (And, though she didn't say it, no more of that dirty Mexican stuff either.) We would be as good as anybody. Better. Culture had found its way to Los Rafas.

All we had to do (she meant me, not we) was to talk to the other girls. There had to be at least ten in order to have the class. As for money—and here was the biggest shock of all—it would be a pittance. I had never before seen Mother cavalier about money. She would add up the bill at the little country grocery store to make sure she wasn't overcharged even a penny, while everybody behind us had to wait. It embarrassed me terribly. I'd move away from her and look in the other direction, pretending that we weren't together. Nobody was fooled.

"Your clothes will be so cute," she said. "Red silk tap pants and a black silk blouse with the school name over the pocket. 'Les Danseuses.' Les Danseuses of Los Rafas."

Well, I've heard worse. "Dance Your Ass Off" for one. The name wasn't important. "Will there be shoes?" I asked, ready to cry if the answer was no.

Mother nodded. "Heather said that as soon as she got the money, she'd send off to Hollywood for everything. In the meantime, she has some used shoes we can buy for rehearsal."

"Hollywood!" I could hardly believe my ears. I was so excited.

"And Heather's going to start an exercise class for the mothers. We'll get leotards in town. I'll be able to lose some weight."

I went dancing through the house, unable to contain my excitement. Mother got on the telephone right away. She called all her friends, who included the ladies in the Altar Society and just about every other woman in Los Rafas.

I finally fell in a heap on the ratty old sofa, breathing hard. Mother was talking to one of her sisters. She was going to lose weight, mucho pounds, and nab this guy at work. This was the first time since Father had died that I heard her mention such a thing.

It was then I realized that Annie Laurie hadn't shown me her father's photograph. I puzzled over her mother's name, Heather. I mean her mother looked like any of the other ladies in Los Rafas. Tan face. Dark hair. Not a hint of red in it. Ladies named Dolores or Juanita or María.

"There he is," Annie Laurie said to me the first day of dancing class.

The photograph was in one of those shiny, gold frames that you get at Woolworth's. The picture was in color too. The first thing I noticed was his bright red hair, just like Annie

Laurie's. Then I noticed with satisfaction that he was not in uniform like my father.

"When did he die?" I asked.

"Oh, he's not dead," Annie Laurie said. "He's in Texas."

I stared at the photograph again. Other than the hair he did not look like Annie Laurie at all. He had a pale, thin face— no freckles. His eyebrows were almost invisible so his eyes popped out like raisins in raw dough.

"He's Scotch," Annie Laurie said, as if she had read my mind.

"Then how come your name is Trujillo?"

"That's my mother's name."

"But how come her other name is Heather?"

Annie Laurie shrugged. "Her real name is Amorosa."

By then the other girls had arrived. Mrs. Trujillo had conjured a record player from somewhere and had put on some music. "All right, ladies," she said, making us feel very grown up. "Let's line up in two rows. First, we're going to learn about rhythm."

Thus began the first of our weekly dancing lessons, followed by practice at home. The goal was to be ready for a recital the first week of May. By then our new shoes and outfits would arrive from Hollywood. Mrs. Trujillo had already talked the school principal into using the multipurpose room; we didn't have an auditorium. At first the recital was going to be on May 5, the Cinco de Mayo, but the mothers nixed that. That might have been OK in Texas, but it wouldn't work with the old-time "Spanish" people of New Mexico. By the time the Mexicans had driven out the French, which was why the Cinco de Mayo was celebrated, New Mexicans had been part of the United States for over twenty years. It was not a holiday we paid much attention to. So it turned into a May Day recital instead.

The next night Mother came home from exercise class exhausted. Her black leotard, the largest size available, wasn't large enough. She bulged here, there, and everywhere, and the poor thing could hardly breathe. I was worried because I had already lost my father, and I didn't want to lose my mother. She waved a flabby arm at me. Just a few pounds, she said, until she regained the figure that she had lost when I was born. That was over nine years ago. I saw how she packed it away at dinner every night. She couldn't blame my birth for all that excess flesh.

That's how it went as winter turned to spring. Mother actually started to lose weight, and Mrs. Trujillo told me I definitely had rhythm—I was going to be a wonderful dancer.

During this time Annie Laurie and I became friends. But she changed toward the end. She seemed remote. I didn't care that much. Sonia Gonzales was still my best friend, and my new tap shoes were coming in the mail from Hollywood any day.

As May approached, Annie Laurie followed me one day after school. "I have to talk to you," she said, looking around to make sure nobody could hear us. "You're my friend, aren't you? I mean we're a lot alike. Neither one of us has a father."

That was just about the cruelest thing she could have said. Deep inside I turned to ice while my face flamed hot with anger. I had never told her anything about my father. Everyone else in class knew that the subject was taboo. How dare she? Who did she think she was?

"You've been nice to me," she said. "You helped me with my math."

Who told you? I wanted to say. Who told you about my father? But I didn't dare speak because I knew I would scream.

"If I'm your friend," I finally said, "why have you been watching me that funny way?"

She gulped and looked away. "Because I thought you knew," she said.

"Knew what?" She continued to look away. "Knew what?" I repeated, raising my voice.

When she didn't answer, I decided to wait her out, staring with one of my mean looks. Finally she said in this little voice, "It's about my father."

What could be so bad about her father? I thought. She told me he wasn't dead. Then I thought of the next worse thing. "He and your mother are divorced," I said. "And they're both going to go to hell."

That got a rise out of her. Her head spun around, and she glared at me. She looked like she wanted to hit me. But she just shook her head quickly that it wasn't so.

"He's not your father at all," I taunted. "He and your mother aren't even married."

Her mouth started to move in that squishy, loose-lipped way like she was getting ready to cry. Suddenly she pressed her lips together and gave me a defiant look. "No," she said very calmly and firmly. "He's in jail."

Well, that snapped the elastic in my bloomers. My mouth fell open, and I was immediately sorry for the mean things I had said to her.

"How come?" I stammered.

"Checks," she said. "Bad checks." Then she turned and ran. She never slowed down a bit, never looked back, not even when the road curved. Then she was out of sight.

After that, even though the recital was less than two weeks away, she didn't talk to me anymore. She drew into herself even though the other girls tried to talk to her—especially those in the dancing class. She didn't pay attention in school, and the teacher scolded her for not getting her math right.

Every once in a while I'd catch her looking at me. I thought maybe her feelings were hurt because she had told me about her father, and I never told her about mine. But she already knew about mine, so what did she have to feel hurt about?

The Saturday before the recital I waited in front of our house by the mailbox. I must have stood there all morning. Finally the mailman drove by in his little red, white, and blue truck. "Nothing today, Becky," he said in Spanish. "Monday for sure."

I didn't know whether to have a fit or to cry. Thursday night was our recital. The parents of our dancing class and the families of the ladies in the exercise class would be there. Plus other people from Los Rafas. It was a real event, a first.

What if the post office didn't deliver our costumes and shoes on time? Dress rehearsal was Tuesday night. I hadn't even seen my outfit or even practiced with anything but beat-up old tap shoes. I had a solo too, and just had to do better than anyone else.

I ran to the back of the house near the chicken coop where Mother was hanging the wash. She had a clothespin in her mouth and grunted at me, shaking her head, while I screamed at her.

When her mouth was free, she screamed right back. "But my shoes," I whined. "My costume. I'll be the only one without."

"Monday," she said. "Wait until Monday. Then we'll see." Grownups have no feeling for what's important.

I suffered agonies the rest of the day, thinking of all the reasons why I'd be the only one without shoes and costume. It would be all her fault. Meaning Mother. I knew it would be her fault for sure when her new boyfriend came to dinner on Saturday. Mother was acting so silly that I wanted to puke. Then they took me to my cousin Rosemary's while they went out dancing. I had a sleepless night, wallowing in doom and gloom, knowing that my life was about to be ruined forever.

The next morning I badgered Rosemary into going to the children's mass. She would rather have pulled the blankets over her head and slept until noon, and she grumbled all the way to church. After mass I headed straight for the girls in our dancing class. I figured all of them would have received their shoes and costumes by now. Surprise! Not a single one had. We looked around for Annie Laurie, but she hadn't come to church yet.

"Maybe everything was going to be sent to Annie Laurie's mother," Sonia said. "Yeah. That's it. She's the one who took the money to order everything. The one who sends the money is the one who gets the stuff—right?"

That made sense. I made Sonia swear on her mother's honor, hope to die, that she would go to Annie Laurie's with me after lunch.

Well, no one was home, not even that ugly, big old car that was a hundred years old and sounded like a cement mixer. Then we went to my house, and I complained to my mother.

"Wait until Monday," she said again. I was tired of waiting, but I didn't know what else to do.

That night I tossed in bed which was really the sofa in the living room. I could hear Mother snoring in the bedroom. In times past when I heard her I thought it was funny, but it wasn't funny this time. I wished that we had one of those clocks that glowed in the dark so I could see when it was midnight. That would be the beginning of Monday which was what I was waiting for. Only there wasn't anything I could do at that hour of the night. If I woke Mother up she would probably whale the dickens out of me.

Finally my eyes got heavy. I was on the verge of sleep when I thought I heard a tap on the living room window. It was such a light tap that it could have been my imagination. It happened a second time. I rolled on my side and stared. The third time I sat up, ready to call Mother. Then I heard the low voice, almost a whisper, through the small window opening.

"Becky. It's me. Annie Laurie."

I tiptoed over and opened the window wider. "Shh," I warned.

"I had to come see you," Annie Laurie said. "You're my friend, aren't you?" I nodded although I wasn't sure I meant it. What can you say to a person who'd ask a dumb question like that through an open window in the middle of the night?

"I just want you to know," Annie Laurie said, "that it's not my fault."

"What's not your fault?"

It was hard to see, even though the moon was bright, but I had the impression that her face had drained of blood.

"We're going," she said.

"What do you mean going?" I was still sleepy and didn't quite understand.

She stood there, her lips pressed tight. "You're my friend," she finally said. "I just wanted to say goodbye. And to say I'm sorry. It's not my fault."

Then she turned and ran into the dark and though I didn't know it then, out of my life.

Well, all hell broke loose at school the next day. Annie Laurie wasn't there, and her desk was empty. She even took the books that belonged to the school with her. The room was abuzz all morning. The teacher pounded her pointer on the desk until it snapped, and she screamed at me for the first time ever.

"Just what is all this, Rebecca? What is going on?"

I told her. But like my mother, she said we should wait and see. At lunch, instead of staying on the school grounds like we were supposed to, Sonia and I sneaked away. We wolfed down our sandwiches as we ran home to check our mailboxes. Nothing. Then we ran to Annie Laurie's house and peeked in the windows. The place was empty except for the few pieces of junky furniture that belonged to the landlord.

We ran back to school. My stomach was queasy, not so much from gulping down my lunch as from the wicked thing that had been done to us.

The school grounds were empty, and we were breathless and sweaty. We hurried into the building and down the hall, trying to be as quiet as we could. I slowly turned the doorknob at the back of our room. When we tiptoed in, the room was even quieter than we were. Everybody had turned around to stare at us. The teacher stood up front, her arms crossed, her lips pressed, and her head nodding. My queasy stomach became a violent roller coaster, and I threw up all over Bennie Romero's desk.

After they cleaned me up, Sonia and I were sent to the principal's office. The principal wrinkled his nose at the faint smell of vomit, but I didn't care. My whole life was ruined. I barely heard his sermon. I kept thinking of my new tap shoes and my costume that I would never see. I kept seeing Annie Laurie at the window, hearing her say, "It's not my fault." But it was! It was!

"I understand your concern, girls," he said. He lisped, which if he had been speaking Spanish might have passed for Castilian. "Maybe they had trouble with their car and were stranded somewhere." He meant Annie Laurie and her mother, but I could tell he didn't believe what he said. It was just more grownup talk. They think that kids are so stupid that we believe any old lie, and that just because we're polite enough to keep quiet that we swallowed their bullchicken.

"The mothers' dance committee will be at rehearsal today. Mrs. Trujillo will be there too. Wait and see." Then he told us we should never have left the school grounds without permission. We could have been kidnapped or run over or something else awful. He was sending a note to our mothers and now we should go back to class.

Well, Annie Laurie and her mother didn't show up for rehearsal. The mothers who were there, those who didn't have daytime jobs, huddled in circles buzz-buzzing about what had happened. Then, after half an hour, the chairwoman sent us home and told us to come back for dress rehearsal Tuesday night.

When Mother came home I spilled my guts. She got on the telephone and all of Los Rafas must have been buzzing with voices of indignant mothers. Some blamed my mother for talking them into it, but Mother ignored them and kept insisting that the show must go on.

It did. With makeshift dance clothes and practice tap shoes. One of the mothers banged away at the piano. The applause was wonderful, maybe because the audience took out its anger at Mrs. Trujillo by clapping their hands until they were red. I only made one mistake in my solo, and the other solos were almost as good.

I never expected to hear from Annie Laurie again, and I didn't want to. But a few months later I got this picture postcard of the Grand Canyon. "We're on our way to Barstow, California, from Gallup. Mamá says they need culture there. I'm sorry. It wasn't my fault." I tore the postcard into a hundred pieces and threw them into the trash.

It was only later, looking back, that I saw the good that came out of it. Mother did lose weight and married my stepfather, who turned out to be very nice. I had been infected with the dancing bug so that when I grew up I started my own folklórico group. When we perform I sometimes check the audience, looking for flaming red hair and wondering whatever happened to Annie Laurie. She's never shown up.

A WHOLE LOT OF JUSTICE

Danny Romero was my best friend. He was a pistol, man, but that was no reason for Tony Medina to kill him. It was a hell of a thing. La gente, the people, marched right from the cemetery down the dirt road all the way to the Río Moreno sheriff's office. Some of us were carrying signs, thrusting them up and down in anger. "Justice!" mine said in big black letters. Others said, "Police brutality!" "Outlaw legalized murder!" Man, you get the scene. People were real mad.

Well, the sheriff came out with three of his deputies. Tony, who was the the fourth one, stayed in the building. I could see him looking out the window, probably pissing his pants. He should have been. Then the town mayor came over from city hall, which is right next door to the county offices and joined the sheriff.

"You can't block the entrance to the building!" the sheriff yelled. His goons, including that dumb brother-in-law of mine, came down the walk and shoved people out of the way. "If you want to march you have to get a permit!" the sheriff yelled. "Now break it up and go home! All of you!"

Then the mayor, old Celedonio Chávez, spoke up to let people know that he was in charge even though he never fools anybody. "The matter is under investigation!" he shouted. "There will be a full report!"

Shit, I thought. Under investigation? What kind of investigation are you going to get when the cops investigate themselves? Another whitewash.

"Power to the people!" one of the young guys in the crowd shouted. There was some pushing and shoving with one of the deputies on the other side of the walk. It looked like the deputy was going to use his club, but he backed off when he found himself surrounded by these angry looking dudes and some of the older women, including Danny's mother.

"All right!" the sheriff shouted. "Break it up!"

It took a while. But after some growling and grumbling and posturing the crowd started to drift away.

I went over to Señora Romero, who was standing next to Danny's girlfriend, Gloria. The señora was a feisty little thing who normally wouldn't take any shit from the police. But this really got to her. Bad enough she's a widow; now she loses a son. And her younger son Roberto, Danny's twenty-year-old brother, is—well, how else can you say it? He's—well, he's simple, see. I don't mean regular dumb but really dumb. God sent him to earth with an angel's smile and the brain of a three-year-old. Poor Señora Romero.

Anyway, I walked her and Gloria and Roberto through town toward Freddie Baca's house. That's where they were having the gathering after the burial. The house is bigger, and Freddie and his wife have a dish antenna so they can get TV from anywhere. They also have one of the few VCRs in town, and we were going to play Danny's tape as part of the memorial.

We passed the tiny Romero adobe; it's just down the block. More family bad luck. The county has threatened to auction it off for back taxes, which is what everybody says started this mess that ended in Danny's death. I know better. It goes back way before that. Some of the vecinas, the neighbor ladies, were crossing the street to the Bacas' house with their plates of tortillas and sopaipillas, their pots of green chile stew and frijoles and posole, and their pans of enchiladas. The minute we walked in, other vecinas in their black widow's dresses came over to Señora Romero and surrounded her like a flock of magpies.

"Hey, Charlie," Freddie Baca called from across the living room. "Come give me a hand with this tape." It was just an excuse. He knew better than me how to work the VCR. Freddie just wanted somebody else to pop open the first beer can and stand around nodding their head while he set the controls.

"Okay, everybody," he said after a few minutes. "We're going to run the program now."

The first ones who came in sat down on the chairs brought over by the neighbors. I saved three in the front row for Señora Romero, Gloria, and Roberto. Some people had to stand or sit on the living room floor, and the rest huddled around the door to the kitchen and the door to the hallway.

"Charlie," Freddie said. "You were his best friend. You wanna say a few words?"

Well, I hadn't expected that. I thought that Freddie would say something, although I should have known better. Or that maybe Father Rivera would say something except that the priest hadn't arrived yet. But what the hell?

"I'm all prayered out," I said. "I just want to remember Danny the way he was. Like on this tape that was on public TV," I said. "He was an artist. And a loving son and brother," I said. "And my best friend." I felt the tears start again so I shut up and nodded at Freddie and sat down on the floor.

The sound came on, and the title flashed on the screen. "Public Television Presents Lowriders of New Mexico. Funded in part by the National Endowment for the Arts. Your local Public Television station. And viewers like you."

Freddie fast-forwarded the tape—there were three interviews on the half-hour program and Danny's was the last one.

Finally there was Danny, bless his soul. Smiling that wicked smile of his. Dressed in his everyday threads—TV was no big deal to Danny. He had on his faded blue jeans and a white T-shirt with a big red chile on the front and the words "Chile Power" in black underneath that you could read when he uncrossed his arms. He was wearing a rolled up blue bandanna across his forehead. He had gone to the barber though, and his hair was trimmed for a change although it hung below his shoulders.

"Danny!" Roberto said as if his brother was really there. Then he turned around and flashed that angel smile of his at everybody.

Danny stood there on the screen in front of his pride and joy, the lowrider that caused the big trouble with Tony Medina. I think he loved that car almost as much as his girlfriend, Gloria.

Some Anglo TV guy asked him some questions about culture and identity and some other bullshit, and Danny gave him a look of disbelief that made everybody in the room laugh.

"Man, this is my baby," Danny said. "This is more than just a car. More than transportation, man. It's like my private chapel. It's a statement."

"Look," he said, walking around the rebuilt 1948 Fleetline Chevy. He stood by the sloping trunk of the lowrider and stretched out his arm to point. "The Virgin of Guadalupe. I airbrushed her myself. I had my brushes blessed in the cathedral in Santa Fe before I started. It's painted there for protection, man. Nobody—I mean nobody—is going to rear-end you when they see the Virgin of Guadalupe staring at them."

"And here," he said, moving around to the hood. Again he stretched out his arm. "Our Lord, Jesus." He made a fast sign of the cross as if he hoped nobody would notice. The camera shot from the back of the car to the front. Jesus' head was up near the hood ornament with His arms outstretched over the front fenders, looking toward the driver's seat. He was in this long white robe and there were rays of golden light shining around His head.

The Sermon on the Mount, Danny said. "Blessed are the poor . . ." And he nodded his head and smiled.

hydraulic system so the front end raised and lowered in time to the salsa music blasting from his car stereo. He cruised it real slow down the dirt road through the center of town like a beautiful battleship or, better yet, like a conquistador parading on his fine Arabian stallion. Man, when you saw that car of his and the way he looked behind the wheel with his woman Gloria beside him, you knew he was the meanest dude in town.

Then the TV guy began interviewing him again, saying something about a cultural art form and ethnic pride and some other stuff I didn't really understand. Finally, he asked Danny how much his lowrider was worth.

"I don't know," Danny said. "I don't go around putting price tags on my life, but it's probably worth more than our house." I know that's for sure, since every cent Danny had went into that car instead of paying the property taxes that were due.

Then the tape was over. "That's it, folks," Freddie said. The people started to stir and head for the kitchen for some food and to talk to each other in low voices, respecting the dead.

I went to the front door and stepped outside to look for Father Rivera. He was coming down the road, waving his arms like he does when he's mad and giving a hell-and-damnation sermon, only this time there was only one parishioner in the audience: the sheriff.

"Bad idea," I said when the sheriff came up to the house.

"See? I told you, damn it!" Father Rivera said.

"It was an accident," the sheriff said. "I want to explain that to everybody."

But I stood in the door and wasn't going to let him in. "We're going to ask for a grand jury," I said. "Then we'll find out if it was an accident."

The sheriff gave me a look like he'd like to lock me up for life plus twenty years. "We don't need any grand jury," he said.

"Give me a badge," I said, "and let me shoot some unarmed drunk and then see what you say." I wasn't thinking of an unarmed drunk but of Tony Medina, off or on duty, armed or unarmed, and I could tell that the sheriff knew what I meant.

The sheriff turned to Father Rivera and flashed him a look that I was impossible. But he sighed, turned back anyway, and looked me straight in the eye. "Tony wants to make amends," he said, "even if it was justifiable." Jesus, I thought. Come on. Legalized murder. "He wants to buy Danny's car. He says maybe it'll help the family out. They need it."

It made me so damn mad I couldn't speak. I glared at Father Rivera, waiting for him to say something, but he stood expressionless and quiet as a church mouse. Where was that hell-and-damnation sermon when you needed it?

"They'll lynch him," I finally managed to say.

The sheriff pretended like he didn't hear, and the padre cleared his throat of something he didn't want to swallow. "You know about the delinquent taxes?" Father Rivera asked. I nodded. "If Danny had paid them like he was supposed to, instead of putting all his money into that Chevy, there wouldn't be this problem," he said.

"This problem is murder," I said, "not taxes. What we want is justice."

The sheriff threw up his hands, spun around on his heels, and headed back down the street. "That car belongs in a museum," I said to Father Rivera. "The Smithsonian or something. Not carrying that son-of-a-bitch Tony Medina."

The padre shook his head as if he'd had enough of me and pushed his way into the house past the crowd that had gathered at the front door.

* * *

Well, the sheriff didn't want any grand jury, that's for sure. He was afraid that all sorts of other shit would come out about the dumb burro way he policed the county, and he would lose his job in the next election. Tony wanted it even less because if the truth came out it was the slammer for him.

In the old days there would have been a feud. One of Danny's friends or family would have gone after Tony and taken care of him. That's the way they used to settle things up here in the mountain villages. As a matter of fact, Gloria put out the word that Tony better not be walking across the road while she was driving her car. Stay out of her way if he knew what was good for him.

Obviously Tony was up shit creek. Nobody but his own family and friends and fellow goons at the sheriff's office would even speak to him. The two things he lusted for, Danny's girl and Danny's car, he couldn't get for love or money. It was his own damn fault, too.

You see, as I said before, it all goes way back. Back to high school when Danny was a sophomore and Tony was a senior. Danny beat him out for first-string quarterback that year, and that planted the seed of hate in Tony. He figured that as a senior it was his turn—and then to get beaten out by a sophomore!

But it was just fate—bad timing—because the next year Coach kicked Danny off the team for insubordination and Tony could have had his first-string job back if he had still been in school. That was the year Danny's old man got killed in that tractor accident, and Danny started raising more hell than usual.

But Danny getting kicked off the team didn't matter to Tony. He never forgave Danny for beating him out the year before. Then there was Gloria.

Gloria was just a little kid when we were in high school and none of us paid any attention to her. By the time she got to high school, Danny and I had somehow managed to graduate and had been working in construction a couple of years.

Anyway, Gloria started to blossom, you know. Really fine. Both Danny and Tony finally noticed her, but she took to Danny right from the first. Danny had this old truck, and he used to pick her up after school when he was off work early or between jobs. They'd cruise down to the drive-in on the highway to Santa Fe for a coke or just hang around Ortega's general store here in town.

By this time Tony had managed to go to community college and study police science. He flunked the test for a job with the Santa Fe police, but damn if he didn't get hired here by the sheriff's department. The sheriff is his uncle.

Anyway, that's when the trouble really started, slowly at first. Gloria wouldn't have anything to do with Tony. Well, you can imagine what that did to him. Here he was a big-shot sheriff's deputy with his spit-and-polish uniform and his shiny sheriff's car, and she wouldn't give him the time of day. Tony figured it was Danny's fault, and that if Danny hadn't been around Gloria would have been his girl. Shows you how dumb that Tony is.

So he started to take it out on Danny. You know, the usual police shit. Double parking. Can you believe that? My God! Double parking is a way of life around here. I mean, you're driving along and you see some friend or maybe one of your cousins, so you just brake the truck and have a nice visit right there in the middle of the road. Nobody in the history of this town ever got a ticket for double parking—until Danny.

Then there was driving too slow. Obstructing traffic, Tony called it. Come on now. There isn't any traffic to obstruct in this two-tortilla town unless somebody's driving a few goats down the road.

Or disturbing the peace. Now that's a good one. Meaning that the radio in Danny's car was too loud.

When he got stopped, Danny's eyes would widen in disbelief, and he would look at Tony all business in his official uniform. "Come on," Danny would say. "What kind of shit is this?"

Tony would recite some law or statute or something with a string of numbers like Danny should be writing them down to look up in the law library in Santa Fe. Then Danny's eyes would get even wider as Tony handed him the ticket. At first

Danny would just throw them in the glove compartment of the truck and forget them. Then later, after he'd had enough chickenshit, he'd take the ticket from Tony, tear it into little pieces, and let the pieces fall onto the ground.

The first big ruckus was when Danny had so many unpaid tickets that they served a warrant for his arrest. That was about the time that he decided he was going to be an artist. He was saving his money to buy this Chevy from some old paisano who never took it anywhere but from home to church and back. Danny wasn't about to pay all the fines and the interest and all the penalties for ignoring the tickets.

Hell, that was the first year he didn't pay the property taxes on the house although he didn't tell his mother. He was looking at ninety days in jail. "Let them give me free room and board for three months," he said. "I can get new seat covers with the money I save." But Gloria wasn't about to let him go to jail, so she paid the fines with the tip money from the restaurant where she worked and then gave him hell. They almost broke up over that.

It was then that Danny started to drink too much. We'd always have a couple of beers, ever since high school. Maybe even have a party over at his place once in a while, and if Tony was on duty, he'd cruise by in his sheriff's car and flash his spotlight on the house for us to quiet down. But hell, we were no louder than any other party, and he never bothered them.

"This is a big county!" Danny would shout out the door. "There are real criminals out there! There's probably a wreck on the main highway. Why the hell aren't you out patrolling your beat?"

Every once in a while, if Danny had had a few too many and was out in public, Tony would run him in for being drunk and disorderly. That's where Danny got his rep for being a bad guy, which he wasn't. It was that damned Tony.

But the real last straw was Danny's lowrider. After Gloria paid his fines, he bought that Chevy. It became a kind of obsession. He was an artist. Not just painting or sculpture or anything like that, but all of them together. A moving sculpture with painting on it, that's how he thought about that car.

He put every extra penny he got into it, not to mention what he could borrow from Gloria. Smoothed out all the imaginary dents he felt as he rubbed his hand along the body. Redid the seats three times to get them just right. Put in that hydraulic system. Then that stereo that made the lowrider a boombox on wheels. The custom car painters weren't good enough for him so he learned how to do it himself. I forget how many coats of lacquer he finally put on it.

Meanwhile, Gloria was waiting not too patiently. "My mother wants to know when we're going to get married," she nagged at him.

"Soon," he said. "Soon as I get this car finished. Then we can get married."

When the car was finished he cruised down the road in that cherry-red Chevy and heads turned. There'd never been anything like it in this town. Or in this county or in all of northern New Mexico. And then being on TV—whew!

Tony couldn't stand it. He wanted that car almost as much as he wanted Gloria. He'd find any excuse to stop Danny and ticket him. It was worse than before. Until that fatal night.

Nobody knows what happened for sure because there weren't any witnesses. The last person to see Danny alive other than Tony was Gloria when he dropped her off at her house. They had been arguing about setting the wedding date, and Danny had had a few too many. "All right," was the last thing he said to her, "I'll tell you when tomorrow." Then he'd driven off in his lowrider.

According to Tony he chased the car halfway across the county after he'd seen it weaving along the road. Finally, the car headed toward town, and it must have run out of gas because it stopped at the turnoff for the highway.

"He was already out of the car and cursing at me when I came out of the patrol car," Tony said. "He reached into the front seat for a weapon and came at me. I thought he had a gun so I pulled my revolver and shot before he did. I didn't mean to hit him in the chest. It was an accident."

Yeah. Everybody in town knows that Danny never owned a gun. When another patrol car and the ambulance finally came, the only things alongside Danny were his car keys and a flashlight. And later when I had the lowrider hauled to Danny's house, I saw the dent on the front fender on the driver's side. A dent like you might make swinging a sheriff's club real hard. That son-of-a-bitch Tony had stopped Danny, banged a dent in his fender, and then shot him when Danny got mad and came at him. It was plain as the nose on your face.

* * *

I don't know what it takes to call a grand jury, but whatever it is we didn't have it. Politics, I say. That sheriff and the judge and the mayor and the county commissioner, they're as thick as thieves. They don't want any scandal to rock their boats. Not that there wasn't already a scandal. Everybody in the county knew about Danny's murder, and a reporter from the Santa Fe paper came up to check it out. The sheriff must have gotten to him because the article turned out to be a tiny paragraph about an unfortunate accident in Río Moreno and it got buried somewhere on a back page.

"They can't do this!" I said to Father Rivera. "There's my best friend out in the cemetery sleeping alongside his father. His poor mother is waiting for the county to auction off her house, and Gloria's probably going to end up an old maid. There's no justice!"

I was thinking that maybe I'd have to take things into my own hands. Get my hunting rifle and go pay that Tony Medina a visit. But Father Rivera must have read my mind.

"Don't do anything rash," he said.

"Don't do anything period!" I said.

"He's already condemned to hell."

"I don't want to wait that long. He ought to pay now!"

"I have a plan," he said. "Give me a few days."

Well, a couple nights later I got this phone call from Señora Romero. She said the sheriff came by and wanted her and me to come down to the station the next morning. Something or other about a release. Release, my ass, I thought. What the hell is that sheriff up to now?

But I couldn't refuse her, so the next morning I called my boss and told him I'd be late for work. Then I picked up Señora Romero and drove her to the sheriff's office. He was all smiles when we walked in. Offered us a cup of fresh coffee instead of that sludge that's usually been sitting on the burner for two days.

"What's all this about a release?" I asked.

He bustled around his desk, shuffling some papers, and fished one out. Then he smiled, he actually smiled—the first time he ever smiled at me—and said, "You were the last one to see Danny Romero's lowrider before that unfortunate accident, weren't you?"

"No!" I said. "It was Gloria Durán."

He kept right on smiling as if he didn't hear me. "I'd like you to sign this affidavit that Danny's car was in perfect shape that day. Then Señora Romero can sign this release."

I smelled a rat. He knew as well as I did that Gloria was the last one other than Tony to see Danny alive. That would make her the last one to see Danny's car. Then I looked down on the desk at the other paper he had his hand on, the release. There was a check made out to Señora Romero right beside it.

"We want someone qualified to judge the condition of the car to sign," he said to me. "Miss Durán does not qualify as an expert."

Expert? What kind of expert do you need to swear that the fender never had a dent in it before that fatal meeting with Tony Medina? I looked at Señora Romero, wondering what this shell game was all about. Then I realized why me instead of Gloria. She probably told the sheriff to shove it when he called her. She probably got so mad she didn't even hear what he had to say. And he knew that I would never refuse to help Danny's mother.

I took another look at the check on the desk. You could fix a dozen fenders with it. You could even—then I got it—even pay off delinquent property taxes. The fix was on.

"All right," I said. "Where? Where do I sign?"

While I was scratching my name onto the affidavit, the sheriff was talking to Señora Romero. "We have a fund to compensate private citizens for damage to their property," he said. "Accepting this check will release us from any further claims. It should more than cover the damage."

He handed her the check, and her eyes popped open wide in surprise. Then he slid the release along the top of the desk.

"Sign it!" I said.

Afterwards, I took her to the bank and then home. Then I drove over to the rectory. Father Rivera must have been waiting for me.

"I wasn't about to let Señora Romero turn down the money," I said. "It saved her house, but it still doesn't make up for Danny."

Father Rivera nodded. "Tony Medina resigned," he said. "He's moving to Albuquerque and taking a job with the Albuquerque police." God help them, I thought.

I stood there, trying to let it all sink in. I stared at the old padre, admiring the way he had performed this miracle. It was really more than I ever expected.

"What did you do?" I asked.

He sort of smiled. "Nothing really," he said. "I just went over to see the sheriff. I reminded him that even though it was another year before election, people had long memories. Then I asked him to help me with a sermon about religion and civic duty that I'm going to give next Sunday, and it didn't hurt that I shared a little gossip with him."

"Gossip?"

"I told him that I heard you were planning to run for sheriff. I heard that you were fixing up Danny's lowrider and were going to go around the county electioneering in it."

"Who told you that?"

He lifted his eyes up to heaven like in those corny Hollywood movies. "Sometimes I hear voices," he said.

Well, shit. I had to burst out laughing. The old fraud. There may not be a whole lot of justice in the world, but at least there's a little. And as for Danny, I'll never forget him. Every time I hear thunder roll over the mountains and across the sky I imagine it's Danny cruising the heavens in his lowrider and looking down at his mother in her little adobe house and smiling.

DEAR ROSITA

Dear Rose,

See. I remember to call you Rose instead of Rosita. Now that you left New Mexico to go to that Eastern university I guess you need a name that fits. So I'll write Rose from now on. Tho your old papá will always think of you as his Rosita.

Mamá says hi. Says now she wishes she had gone to school so she could write to you. Except times were hard then. She had to go to work almost as soon as she learned to walk. But she's glad times are better now and *you* can go. The first one in the family to go to college. She's very proud of you. With your scholarship and everything. She shake her fist and say, "Show 'em, Rosie. Show 'em what kinda stuff Sandoval women are made of."

Sometimes at night I catch her leaning on the adobe wall and staring out the window with tears in her eyes. "Where's Massachusetts?" she say. "Do the pilgrims still live there? And how about that madam on the boat?" she say. "The *Mayflower.* Mrs. González tole me about that. That's not very nice."

I tell her not to worry. You're not going on any boat. You're at the university.

Your little brothers and sisters say hello and send you kisses. They say to send them a souvaneer from back East. They ask, "Is your university in one of those tall buildings like on TV? Do the people live in those tall buildings too? Where do they keep the chickens and the goats? (Hah!) And how can you get any sunshine if you're always indoors and there are no fields?"

The kids have been very good since you been gone. The corn crop was so big that they worked extra hard this year. Panchito picked more than anybody. Almost as much as a man. And he sold at our stand all by himself when I had to take Mamá to the doctor.

Well, that's all for now. I got to go out to the corral and feed the animals.

Love,
Papá

*   *   *

Dear Rose,

We receive your letter. We think it very funny that the woman at the university post office said you had to pay extra to send the T-shirts because she didn't think New Mexico was in the United States. At least I think it funny. Mamá got mad. "What kind of dumb university is that where they don't know their states?" she say. "How they going to teach our daughter anything?"

Panchito's teacher say there is a magazine here called *New Mexico*. The state prints it. Every month there is a page called "One of Our Fifty Is Missing." It tells about other dumb people who don't know where New Mexico is. They think it Old Mexico which is another country.

The kids are crazy for the T-shirts with the university name on the front. Everybody at their school is jealous. Sometimes they play like they go to university like their big sister. It must cost a lot to buy eight T-shirts. I know you have this job in the Affirmative Action office at school. But you say you have to read six hours a day for your homework. So either you can't work too much and earn money. Or you don't sleep enough which is not healthy. Or those smart professors found how to stretch the day to 28 hours. Anyway, there was lots of corn this year. We earned a little extra so am sending you a money order to help with the T-shirts.

How was your Thanksgiving there in the land of the pilgrims? Around here the Indians don't eat much turkey but corn and chile and frijoles like us. Or cabrito. There is nothing so good as bar-b-q goat. But we roasted some chickens this year. And the corn was so sweet and tender.

I am sorry you can't come home for Xmas. It will be the first time ever we won't all be together. We'll hang out your stocking and save it for you when you come home next summer. Santa won't forget his Rose.

Well, time to open the sluice gate to the acequia. It has been dry so we need to fill the ditch with more water from the Río Grande.

Love,
Papá

* * *

Dear Rose,

What's all this about I'm not supposed to eat meat? All my life I was too poor to buy much meat. I mean like round steak or roast. Now that things are better and we can afford beef, there's all this worry about your heart. Don't eat meat! You say we suppose to eat fish. But tell me. You grew up here in Los Rafas. You know it's desert. Where you going to get fish in the desert? Sure, we could go up north in the mountains and fish for trout. It's only an hour by car. But who has the time even if your car is running OK? There's too much to do on our little plot of ground.

Not only that. Now I hear that beans are *good* for you. Lots of protein. Very high fiber too. So you can go to the excusado regular. Any fool could have told you that. Then some smart doctor says that chile is good for the blood. Cleans out the fat or something. Another smarty doctor says we need more exercise.

More exercise? I bet he never did anything harder than push pills. Just send him down to the country to work the land for a summer. He'll know what exercise is. Who needs to go out and run on purpose? Or sweat and breathe hard on purpose? Man, that's the way we *live*—sweating and breathing hard.

So here I am. Practically an old man who spent his life on the land, one of the working poor. I've had a little luck so I can enjoy my old age, and now what? They tell me: Don't give up chile and beans for steak and potatoes. Continue to work like a dog in the fields. Do all that and you live longer. Maybe not happier but longer. Like the Bible say, if you wait long enough the seasons change and everything comes back to you. Who needs it?

Anyway, I got to go out in the field and sweat again so I can live to a ripe old age.

Love,
Papá

*   *   *

Dear Rose,

That was very interesting what you write us about the Big Bang. When I first mentioned Big Bang your mamá got real mad. "Is that what they teach her at those Godless universities—" she say, "how to talk dirty?"

Then I explain to her that it's not dirty at all. It's just science. These guys with big brains, they sit around figuring how things work. Like how the world began. And the Big Bang was at the beginning of time when everything exploded and made the earth and stars and everything.

"Explosions?" she say. "Hah! Any fool knows that when things blow up they break apart into a million pieces. So how can that be the beginning of the world with things breaking apart? Those professors been sitting around in their rooms so long that all the blood drained to their butts. They gone loco. Like old Señora Armijo who thinks that she flies through the

desert when she falls asleep at night. When you don't know
the dream from the real thing, you're in big trouble."

Then she look at me with that look that could scare the
devil himself. "And anyway," she say. "What about Adam and
Eve? You think they gonna live through any explosion?
Explain that to me, smart guy. Tell that to the priest the next
time you go to confession."

Well, you know your mamá. The best thing is to shut up
and give her a couple a days to cool off. Anyway, I don't understand this Big Bang thing enough to argue with her. So I went
out to the corral and read your letter again.

Mamá had a good point. What about Adam and Eve? And
the apple and the snake? It wouldn't take much of a bang for
them to be blown to pieces. But even more important, hija. Do
you still go to church? I hope you don't let all this science and
all this smart talk turn you away from God. Next thing you
know you'll be joining the zoo keepers who tell us we came
from monkeys. Although sometimes, like with your mamá's
older brother, your Uncle Luis, I wonder. Anyway, please.
Don't turn away from God. Remember to go to mass every
Sunday and holy day of obligation. And say your prayers every
morning and night. We want you to come back to us the same
sweet daughter who left.

I'm gonna go and say a little prayer for you right now. God
bless you. And be smart, but not so smart that you forget God.

Love,
Papá

* * *

Dear Rose,

What's all this about bail? I didn't tell your mamá because I
knew it would break her heart. Not only are you the first in the
family to go to college, your the first to need bail.

I don't understand why anybody has to take over the university president's office. Any fool knows that those big shots

got the cops on their side. The little guy hasn't got a chance. If the cops aren't enough, they can call out the marines. Or—like Panchito say—they nuke 'em.

Anyway, what is this nonsense about bail? Of course we would have sent it if you had asked, but you didn't. So who paid for you? How you gonna pay the money back? Especially if they fire you from your job because of taking over the big shot's office. I don't know, hija. Sometimes I think you're too smart for your own good.

Anyway, it didn't make the newspapers here so you don't have to worry about that. Nobody knows but me, and I won't tell even if they cut my tongue off.

I know I'm not an educated man. But there's some things I learn just by living. And one of them is to never bite the hand that feed you. I mean like scholarships and things. Another is, you can't fight city hall. Which means don't take over the president's office.

Sure. I know how you feel that there aren't enough Chicano and Black and Chinese professors. Everybody like to see some of their own kind make good. Have a professor who understands what you come from and how hard you worked for it. How much you want a chance like everybody else. But Rose, you got to do these things the right way.

What you do now, Rose, is make an appointment with this president. Go see him and have a nice talk. Be honest with him. If he the right kind of guy, he will understand. If he don't understand, do what we did in the fields when a skinflint farmer don't pay a living wage. The crops, they just come up once a year. You don't pick at the right time—boom! There goes every red cent you planned to harvest. Well, colleges are like that too. Only their crops are students. They're student farms. And if a farm don't turn out crops, they don't make money. If they don't make money, they get a new farmer or the banks take over the farm. I don't want to sound like no revolutionary, but that's how I see it. It worked in the fields. Maybe it will work in the colleges. It's something you can do without getting arrested. Which means you don't have to pay bail.

Anyway, the goats are making a racket in the corral. They say they go on strike if I don't feed them. Everybody wants something from somebody. That's all for now.

Love,
Papá

* * *

Dear Rose,

I been thinking about bail since the last time I wrote. Lots of good people been put in jail. Jesus. That Indian man Gandhi. I don't remember who else, but lots of good people. I don't know if George Washington ever got arrested, but I bet if those red coats had got him they'd have locked him up for life plus a hundred years.

What reminded me was cleaning out the old shed. You didn't know but we going to make a room from it and cut a door into the rest of the house. We need another room to separate the boys and the girls. They getting older, and it's the right thing to have a room for the boys and another for the girls.

Anyway, I found these old newspapers. Some of them go way back. This was before your time, and I'm sure you don't remember it. But there was that big land problem up north in Tierra Amarilla maybe 20, 25 years ago. The people, they got into a—I don't know what you call it. Maybe a war. With the government. About who the land belong to and who can do what to it.

Anyway. There on the front page is this big picture. This paisano with his cow. The cow is staring over the barb wire fence. And the farmer, he got tears in his eyes and he say: "My cow, she got arrested." Alongside the cow—her name was Dolores—was this government chota, shiny badge, holster with gun and all, holding a rope. The other end was around Dolores's neck.

Seems like Dolores, she a naughty girl. She go through a broken place in the fence into this field that say "U.S. Government. No Trespassing." But Dolores, she can't read. So this cop, he tie a rope around her neck and arrest her. I wonder if he read her her rights? And the poor old farmer, he has to pay the bail. Or maybe it was a fine. Anyway, I wonder if they really put that cow in a cell? Sounds pretty silly to me. Specially since the fence was broke, and how's a cow supposed to know? Just one of God's dumb creatures.

So I guess you not in bad company. Jesus. Gandhi. Maybe George Washington. And Dolores the cow. Only don't let it happen again if you can help it. Someday somebody may not have the bail.

That's all for now. I promised to take Mamá to church tonight. We say a prayer for you.

Love,
Papá

✱ ✱ ✱

Dear Rose,

Oh, how sad we all were that you may stay and work back East this summer. It seems so long since we see you. Tina start to cry, and then your Mamá. Pretty soon everybody. So it was like a flood in the house. The linoleum in the front room had tear spots all over. We hardly talked. Just worked. At supper we could not look in each other's eyes. Then your next letter came that said you were coming home. Everybody start to smile and laugh again.

Don't worry about the money. If you don't find a job here, we will help you. Money isn't everything. I mean you need enough to get along. But whether you eat beans or steak don't matter as long as you eat. (And I learn from you this year that beans are better.) Money you can always earn. But not seeing your friends, not seeing your family. That's something if you miss, you never get back. Your little brothers and sisters grow so much since you went away. You'd hardly know them. Now Panchito, he say he going to college too. They all so proud of their big sister and want so much to see you.

Your mamá have this fear. She say, "How am I going to talk to her? I never talk to no college person except when I go to the doctor. What am I going to say? What if she's changed? Is she going to be ashamed of her mamá who can't even write her a letter? Oh, I'm so worried."

Worry, worry, worry. She worry you don't come. She worry you *do* come. I just say, "Relax. Just tell her you love her. She the same daughter you used to nurse and change diapers and all that. She still learn a thing or two from you. So don't worry. It'll be fine. Besides. I bet she can't cook like you. Not yet."

But the truth is, I worry a little too. We are so proud of you. And want you not to be ashamed of us poor country folks. You are going up in the world. Only like the old story: Don't get too close to the sun or it melt your wings and down you go.

Look for us at the station when your bus comes in. Panchito nag his sisters and brothers to wash and iron their university T-shirts. That's so you can tell who they are because they grown so much since you gone. They think you be a grown lady like a princess in the movies now that you been in the university one year. They are so excited.

God love you and speed you home safely. We are so excited our hearts will burst. So hurry home. We can hardly wait to see you next week.

With love from all,
Papá

THE BORDER

"There is no border between Los Estados Unidos and México," the raspy voice said to Pablo in a dream. "It is all one land, no matter how many fences are built along an imaginary line. The border is a superstition that true sons of the ancient land do not accept."

Pablo groaned. He could see the old, white-haired coyote sitting on its haunches, its mouth curved back in its sharp snout as if it was smiling. "Go away," he said in his dream. "Leave me alone."

The old coyote's mouth curved even more, and its yellow eyes gleamed. "You have to go back," the coyote said. "Your father is dying. He wants to give you your inheritance."

"Sweat is my inheritance," Pablo said. "Sweat and hunger and poverty. I already have more of those than I need."

"Your father is dying. He's calling for you."

Pablo pulled the thin blanket over his shoulders. He rolled onto his side, jostling his two little brothers, and faced the wall so he would not have to look at the coyote. But he forgot that the walls in dreams are transparent, and he could still see the old pest looking at him.

This time though, Coyote did not speak. Instead he lifted his head, pointed his snout toward the stars, and began to howl. It was the usual coyote howl except for the rasp that sounded as if he needed cough medicine. The old busybody had either been howling too much at what was none of his business or smoking too many cigarettes.

The more Coyote howled, the darker it grew, as if dawn could not stand the irritable sound of his voice. All Pablo could see was the yellow gleam from Coyote's eyes. Then it began to grow light, and the moon gradually came into view, beaming its golden shimmer on the earth.

Maybe the man in the moon will tell this loudmouth to shut up so I can have some peace, Pablo thought, not realizing that the moon might have come in answer to Coyote's call. When he looked, Pablo did not see a man in the yellow sphere. What he saw instead was a large hacienda whose walls dissolved to show a bedroom that was as rich and beautiful as a cathedral.

Three votives in a nicho illumined a statue of the Virgin. The tiny flames were so intense that their reflection on the silver crucifix above the bed lit the room as if it were daylight. And there, from under silk sheets as white as clouds, a figure turned and stared at him.

"Hijo," the man said. "Where are you, hijo?"

Pablo did not recognize him. It had been years since he had seen his father, years since his mother had divorced him because she did not want to return to Mexico.

"Here a woman is more than a goat or a pig or a burro!" the four-year-old Pablo had overheard her shout in anger. "More than a piece of property! Here I am a person!" Then the sharp sound of flesh striking flesh, the stifled cry, and Mamá was dragging him by the hand from the shack at the edge of the patrón's field. He never saw his father again.

Pablo's brow furrowed over questioning eyes as he stared at the man in the bed. The white-haired, emaciated figure was old enough to be his grandfather. The man looked at him just as questioningly. After all, it had been twelve years.

"Father?"

The old man's face brightened with hope. "Hijo?"

Then the vision in the moon faded, and Pablo lay awake, trembling and cold. "I have to go," he thought to himself. "I have to." The coyote's howl, now distant, echoed in his head.

He did not tell his mother the next morning. He knew she would say no. As for his stepfather, Armando, he would probably say good riddance, one less mouth to feed. There were four other children, all younger than Pablo, including his two half-brothers with whom he shared the pallet on the floor of the trailer.

He waited two days so he could collect his pay from the fast-food restaurant where he worked. Most of that went into the family coffers, but he had been permitted to keep a little for himself that, over the months, he had saved.

"Dear Mamacita," he wrote. "Don't worry. I'm a grown man now. I can take care of myself. I had a vision that my blood father was calling to me. He's dying. I have to go to him. Hug my little brothers and sisters for me and tell Armando that I'll be back to help as soon as I can. I already told them at work. Your loving son, Pablo."

Then, straw bag in hand for a suitcase, he walked out of town toward Interstate Highway 25, heading south toward the border.

* * *

"You don't look from around here," the Navajo driving the pickup truck said. "What pueblo you from?" Pablo shook his head. The driver studied his face. "Mojado?" he asked.

Pablo flushed. "I was born in Hatch."

The Navajo grinned. "A chile picker," he said as if that confirmed his guess.

"American," Pablo said.

"Yeah," the Navajo said as if he didn't quite believe it. "Me too. Where you headed?"

"El Paso."

"The asshole of the Río Grande," the Navajo said. "Maybe even the asshole of the West. Albuquerque's better." Then the Navajo studied him again, wondering. "How come you left Santa Fe? Now there's a town."

Pablo shook his head, remaining silent. The Navajo grinned. "You sure you're not one of those pueblo dudes? You're about as talkative as they are."

Pablo shook his head and stared straight in front at the unfurling black ribbon of highway.

* * *

Pablo stood at the turnoff to Los Lunas when he swore he saw the white coyote. He had turned to watch the pickup truck as it sped toward town when he thought he saw the animal out of the corner of his eye. It was sitting on a slight rise of desert watching with a stupid grin on its face.

Pablo turned abruptly toward the highway and raised his thumb at an approaching automobile. When the automobile passed, still going seventy miles an hour, he sneaked a look over his shoulder. There was nothing there. But as he walked along the edge of the highway, he could feel its presence behind him. Before him in all directions was the desert. Above him was the sky bleached by the intensity of the sun.

After a while he put down his bag, took off his visored Dallas Cowboys cap, and wiped his brow. He removed the plastic water bottle from the bag, uncapped it, and tilted back his head to take a sip. A black bird circled so high above that he couldn't tell whether or not it was a buzzard or whether or not it was following him.

"What am I doing?" he thought. "I could have taken the bus to El Paso. I would still have enough money for the buses in Mexico."

Ahead and to the west, some distance from the highway, a bluff rose from the desert floor, casting a thin strip of shadow that beckoned. But the highway also beckoned, and Pablo turned toward the sound of an approaching automobile, ready to raise his thumb.

* * *

"You from around here, kid?" the waitress asked in Spanish. She meant Belen.

"I was born in Hatch."

"Driving home, huh?" Pablo shook his head and gave a hitchhiking gesture with his fist and raised thumb. "You gotta be kidding." She set the glass of iced cola and the check in front of him and gave him a look as if he was some kind of nut.

Pablo watched her return to the other end of the counter where she had been talking to the only other customer in the cafe. They were looking at him and nodding their heads when the short-order cook shouted in English, "Pick up!"

The waitress took three steps toward the window to the kitchen and lifted a plate from the counter. "Where's the pota-to chips?" she bawled. "And the extra pickle?"

Pablo gulped down the cold drink, leaving the ice in the glass. He didn't like the way they had been looking at him. He knew that he looked young for his age. They probably figured he was a runaway.

He left the money on the counter on top of the check and hurried out the door. He was thankful he had gone to the bathroom first, rinsing his face and filling the plastic water bottle. He hurried across the small parking area and headed toward the highway, walking rapidly to put distance between himself and the town.

Pablo was a mile south when he heard a van cruising down the road. He turned and raised his thumb, waiting hope-fully. As it slowed to a stop he read the words on the side, "La Golondrina Imports and Exports."

"Climb aboard, kid."

Pablo opened the door and hopped in. The white man's face was weathered from the sun, tufts of grizzled hair poking out from under his soiled Stetson. A cowboy.

"I'm going right by Hatch," the man said. He put the van in gear, squinted out the side-view mirror, and rolled out onto the highway. When he heard the word, Hatch, Pablo recognized the customer from the cafe.

The cowboy looked over and grinned when he saw Pablo's expression. "That María," the man said, "she's a regular good Samaritan, busybody, whatever. Long as somebody else has to do the work. Hatch, huh?"

Pablo wasn't sure what to answer. Finally he said, "El Paso. I'm going to El Paso."

"I thought you was born in Hatch."

"I was. But I'm going to El Paso."

"Well, you're in luck. I hit all those towns from El Paso to Santa Fe and back. Albakirk. Belen. Socorro. Truth or Consequences. Las Cruces. El Paso. Even Juárez sometimes."

The man reached over and flicked on the radio. Reba McEntire joined them, singing an old song about not wanting to be a one-night stand.

✳ ✳ ✳

It was dark by the time they drove into El Paso. The freeway ran through the long strip of a city with lights in the hills on both sides.

"Where you want off, kid?" the cowboy asked. Pablo did not know, and when he didn't answer, the man looked at him suspiciously. "You got family here?"

"No." His voice sounded as small and lonesome as he felt.

"Well, where you going?"

"Mexico."

"Mexico, huh?" The cowboy looked at him as if trying to figure out why and shook his head. He turned the van off the freeway at the next turnoff, then pulled over to the curb at the first chance. "The civic center's that way," he said, pointing toward the south. "The bridge over the river's that way too. Just cross the bridge and there you are."

"Thank you, Mister."

Pablo stood and watched the van drive back toward the freeway. Then he turned and looked at the tall buildings and the city lights, feeling more lonesome than ever. It looked even bigger than Albuquerque.

✲ ✲ ✲

He did not know the name of the park. At least he thought it was a park. His tired feet led him there. He picked a spot deep in the shrubbery where no one could see him, and he lay on the ground and fell asleep. That was when the coyote came back to him.

"You should have asked the cowboy for some money," the coyote said, speaking in Spanish now. "He would have given it to you."

"Go away," Pablo said in his dream. "I'm tired. I don't want to talk to you."

The coyote grinned. "I've been following you all the time. Who do you think has been your protector?"

"I don't need a protector," Pablo said. "I have my patron saint." He rolled over on his other side, his back to the coyote, and closed his eyes tighter.

"You don't have any cigarettes, do you?" the coyote asked.

"You smoke too much. You sound like you've already wrecked your throat. Now shut up and leave me alone."

There was a rustle in the bushes and Pablo turned and opened his eyes a slit. Standing on the end of a branch that sagged almost to the ground was a jet black crow, the biggest crow he had ever seen.

"Don't listen to this smooth talker," the crow said. "He's a liar and a cheat."

"What are you doing here?" the coyote said. "You're not a desert bird. You're out of your territory."

The crow eyed the coyote and gave him the crow's version of the "bird," a loud caw.

"Cornfield thief," the coyote said. "Chicken with a black dye job." Then to Pablo, "Who was it that brought you a message from your father?"

"Wait until he presents you with the bill," the crow said. "Everything he does has strings attached to it. More strands than a spider's web. Beware."

Then the crow spread his wings and flapped off into the dark, and the branch on the bush snapped back into place.

"I can show you across the Río Bravo," the coyote said. "I can help you find your father's village."

"Good night," Pablo said. Then it was blackness. In his dream he had finally fallen asleep.

✳ ✳ ✳

The next morning he followed the crowd over the bridge into Ciudad Juárez. Since he looked like he belonged, the guards just waved him through. He had never been in Mexico before, and he stared around himself in amazement. Everything seemed slightly off-center, as if he were peering through glasses that were out of focus.

The adobe buildings were familiar, similar to those on the north side of the river, but still they looked different, like photographs he'd seen of buildings in Santa Fe a hundred years ago. In need of repair. Not quite refined. The streets, though crowded, were narrower. And though he had spoken Spanish all his life, it seemed strange not to hear the poetic flow interrupted by the more abrupt and direct sound of English.

"¡Joven!"

The call, spoken over the noisy bustle, merged with other crowd sounds.

"Young man!" This time in accented English.

Pablo looked up, surprised to see a man staring at him. There was something familiar about the crooked smile and the arrogant bearing. The black hair did not go with the wrinkled face. It reminded him of the prune-faced little old Spanish ladies he saw in church in Santa Fe on Sundays with jet black hair that was too obviously dyed. Their heads hadn't seen a real black hair in twenty years.

The man dropped a half-smoked cigarette onto the sidewalk and ground it out with the sole of his shoe. He shot an appraising glance at the straw bag that Pablo carried.

"How can I be of service, young man?" he asked.

Pablo shook his head.

"Reasonable rates by the hour. I can do anything. Guide you . . . anywhere." He smiled his crooked smile and thrust into Pablo's hand a business card that read: "Don Juan Zorro. Expert guide. Credit on approval."

Pablo walked on, not looking back, searching for the bus station. An hour later he was on his way, seated on the rearmost seat next to an old woman carrying a birdcage on her lap. "Tortillas y frijoles," the small green parrot said. "Gusanos y lechuga." Pablo pulled the brim of his cap down over his eyes and went to sleep, but this time he did not dream.

* * *

The farther from the border, the rougher the road became, except when they approached big cities, where the road got smoother and wider. They drove through high desert country to Chihuahua, then dropped down to Torreón. After that they started to climb into high mountains. The old woman and her parrot had long since left, and a shy young Indian couple had squeezed into her place, heading all the way to Mexico City.

Pablo had never seen so many big cities. He stayed close to the bus at meal stops, afraid that it might leave without him.

Late in the afternoon of the third day the bus bumped to a stop at a crossroad that led up into the mountains. "El Pueblo de los Parados!" the driver said, walking to the back of the bus and shaking Pablo awake.

Half asleep, Pablo picked up his bag and followed the driver to the door. He looked through the windshield and turned to the driver in alarm. "There's nothing here," he said.

The driver shrugged. "That way." He pointed toward the dirt road that angled off the main highway.

Pablo turned toward the other passengers, looking for confirmation. But their faces stared blandly ahead or out the side windows, except for the young Indian couple who smiled at him.

"Up in the mountains," the driver said.

Pablo dismounted from the bus. "How far?" he asked.

"Twelve kilometers."

The door slammed shut, and the bus groaned down the paved highway, belching exhaust. Pablo turned and stared at the countryside. It was growing darker now that the sun was setting over the tops of the mountains.

Twelve kilometers, he thought. That's—He tried to remember how far twelve kilometers was. Seven miles! Then he started walking along the dirt road that soon became a trail leading to nowhere.

*   *   *

After an hour it was so dark that Pablo could barely see the way. He could tell that he had been climbing because of the pull in his calves.

He stopped and looked around. Above, stars gave off what little light there was. A thin, curved thread of a moon shone feebly. The silence unnerved him. He would have preferred the cries of wild animals to the silence, a silence in which dangerous things lurked watching him.

Then, in sheer fatigue, he forced himself from the road into the brush, no longer caring what might be waiting there. He found a clearing and sank to the ground. That night, for the first time since he had boarded the bus, the coyote came to him in his dreams.

"You should have listened to me back in Juárez," the coyote said. "I would have guided you. You would have been there by now."

"I didn't see you in Juárez," Pablo said. The coyote grinned as if he knew a secret. "Besides, what could you have done differently?"

"Picked your pocket," came a voice from the dark. Then the crow cawed in what for him was a laugh.

"Get lost, piñón breath," the coyote said. "This is none of your business."

Pablo did not understand what was happening. Where did the crow fit into all this? It was because of the coyote that he had set out to find his father. Yet the coyote made him uncomfortable, while the crow cautioned him to be careful.

"Climb on my back," the coyote said. "I can carry you into the village where you can claim your birthright."

"For a fee," the crow said. "Ask old peludo about the fee."

Pablo turned to the coyote, who was staring maliciously at the crow. If crow had been tasty, the coyote would have eaten him right there.

"I'm sleepy," Pablo said. "And I'm tired of you two arguing every time I try to get some rest." Then, in his dream, he fell asleep, and the coyote and crow disappeared—pop!—just like that.

＊　＊　＊

Pablo was awake at first light. He rinsed his mouth, drank the last of the water from the plastic bottle, ate two of the tortillas that he had bought at a bus stop, then set out on his way.

An hour and a half later he heard the barking of dogs coming from just over the crest of the trail. He stopped to catch his breath, not so much from the climb as from excitement. He was approaching his mother's and father's village. His village.

His mother had seldom spoken about Los Parados, which meant The Unemployed, saying only that it had been a rich mining area when her grandfather had been a young man. She seldom spoke about what it had been like to grow up in a Mexican village in the mountains. It was as if she had never been a girl, but had been born full grown, a wife and mother scrubbing floors, cooking, working in the fields. Yet from his dreams Pablo knew that it was someplace special. He saw once again the hacienda in the moon and his father in bed between white silk sheets, beckoning to him.

When he started walking, a pack of dogs appeared at the crest, wagging their tails and barking. They were a skinny bunch, ribs visible through mangy fur. He squatted to pick up a dried stick, standing quickly as he grasped it firmly in his hand. The dogs stopped barking and stood watching. One of them came forward, wagging its tail and wiggling its body, sniffing to see what he had in his straw bag.

As he reached the crest, a young girl and a white-haired old woman stood by the side of the trail watching. "Who are you?" the old woman asked. "You don't belong to this village."

* * *

Pablo wasn't sure whether to feel like the grand marshal leading a parade or a prisoner herded along by a lynch mob. The old woman and girl walked on either side of him. The pack of dogs followed, yelping excitedly as they marched down the slope into the village.

Everyone in the village must have emptied the few dozen little houses to watch. They were old people for the most part, more women than men, with several dirty grandchildren staring silently.

The old woman and girl guided Pablo toward an adobe casita on the edge of the barren plaza where an old man in a sombrero sat on a wooden chair tilted back and leaning against the wall.

"He looks like he comes from here," one of the women in the plaza said.

"Jefe," the old woman escorting Pablo said. "A stranger."

* * *

"All the men who are young enough and able enough to work are gone," El Jefe said, "to El Norte. Some of their women too. They come back once a year at the time of the village fiesta.

"Ramón Barreras?" El Jefe shrugged. "He left twenty years ago. He and his young wife. To los Estados Unidos." El Jefe studied Pablo's features. Finally he said, "You look like your father."

Pablo could hear the whispers from the crowd surrounding them. "Es chicano," someone said. "No es mexicano."

"Es gringuito," another whispered. "Puro pocho. He can't even speak proper Spanish."

Pablo flushed in embarrassment. This was his father's village. His mother's village. How could they say such things about him? He decided to ignore the whispering.

"He never came back?" Pablo asked.

El Jefe stared into the sky as if trying to remember. Then he looked at the old woman who had brought Pablo to him. "Two, three years ago," the woman said. "When his mother died. He stayed for a while. That was the last time."

"Are any of my father's people left?" El Jefe shook his head. "And my mother's people, los Castillos?"

"All gone. Except those who chose to stay permanently." El Jefe pointed a gnarled finger to a gently sloping hillside sprinkled with weathered wooden crosses and crude headstones.

I came all this way for nothing, Pablo thought in shock. He looked at the gathering of villagers who were listening to their conversation. The children barefoot in rags, holding on to wrinkled grandparents' hands. The small adobe hovels with no running water or electricity.

"But the hacienda?" Pablo said. "In my dream I saw my father in the hacienda."

"You passed it on the trail from the highway," El Jefe said. "But you have to know where to look. Some Norteamericanos own it now."

There was a tittering from the crowd. As if they were amused that a Norteamericano would want to live in such an out-of-the-way place.

* * *

The villagers shared their midday meal with Pablo and asked him questions about El Norte, questions that their own sons and daughters could not answer. Then El Jefe himself rode Pablo back toward the highway, the two of them on a bony horse.

"There," El Jefe said, pointing down a dirt road that branched off from the trail. "You can see the wall where the property begins. There's a path from the gate to the buildings." The old man turned his horse back toward the village and waved. "Buena suerte, Chicanito."

Minutes later Pablo stood outside the locked iron grill gate. Inside he could see the tracks of automobile tires along the path to the large house. The house looked newly plastered and the grounds well cared for, as if someone lived there and had gone away for the day.

"I'll wait," he said to himself. "I have to." So he found a place in the shade and leaned against the wall to rest. Soon he had nodded off to sleep.

* * *

"Here's where you will find your birthright," Coyote said. "In the hacienda."

"Beware," the crow cautioned.

"Lots of pesitos," the coyote said. "Remember who told you about it."

"Hah!" the crow said. "What good are pesitos to a coyote?"

The coyote gave the crow a dirty look but did not respond. Instead he turned to Pablo. "Anyone who helps you find something of value is entitled to a finder's fee," he said. "It's the unwritten law."

"Go away," Pablo said. "Leave me alone."

"Remember," the coyote said.

"To thine own self be true," said the crow.

✳ ✳ ✳

Pablo thought he was still dreaming when he sensed the glare of headlights and heard the sound of an automobile. He smiled at the thought that either the coyote or the crow was driving. His dreams were getting more preposterous all the time. But when he heard the iron gate clang and the sound of the automobile fade, he realized that he must be awake. He opened his eyes and saw that it was very dark and must be very late. He would have to wait until morning. So he closed his eyes and drifted back to sleep.

The next morning he was awakened by the sound of hoeing on the other side of the wall. Quietly and carefully he stood and stretched, then picked up his bag and sneaked away toward a tree that hid him from view. He drank from his water bottle and hungrily gulped down the last of his tortillas. Then he sat on the ground, staring at the wall, trying to decide when would be the right time to go.

✳ ✳ ✳

The woman looked up when Pablo opened the gate and stood looking in. "John?" she said. Then Pablo saw the man, squatting, stick his head out from behind a shrub. "We have a visitor," the woman said.

The man stood, and the woman lowered her hoe so that the blade rested on the ground. They looked like Norteamericanos all right, Anglos as he would have called them in Santa Fe. Old people. Maybe fifty or sixty years old. But still healthy looking, like people with money. They looked at Pablo as warily as he looked at them.

"Hello," Pablo said. "I'm looking for my father."

The man and woman looked at each other, the woman visibly relaxed now. "Oh," she said to her husband. "He speaks English."

The man pushed back the brim of his straw hat and approached the gate. "Is he one of the workmen from the village?" the man asked. "Nobody's working today."

Pablo shook his head. He thought of telling them about his dreams, but they did not look like the kind of people who believed in those kinds of dreams. Instead he said, "I came from Santa Fe."

The man and woman exchanged glances again. "New Mexico?"

Pablo nodded. "My father and my mother came from here," he said. "His name was—is—Ramón Barreras."

The man and woman looked at each other once more, only this time her expression was different. As if she was searching her memory.

"Ramón . . . ," the woman said, her voice trailing off softly. She looked at Pablo, studying his face, then turned back toward her husband. "When we first came. Remember? About two years ago." She looked at Pablo once more. "He was in his early forties. His hair was prematurely gray, almost white."

"I don't know," Pablo said in a small, embarrassed voice. "I haven't seen him in years."

"So you've come back home," the man said. "Is that it?"

Pablo was not sure how to answer. "I came to find my father," he finally said.

"You look like him," the woman said. "Yes. I can see the resemblance. Except for the hair. He—John—wasn't he going to Texas? It seems to me he was going to Texas."

Pablo listened as the couple talked back and forth, reminding each other, unearthing the past. He tried to conjure up the man with the white hair from the back and forth of their recollections.

The man was staring thoughtfully at Pablo. "He worked for us that spring," he said. "He had come back for his mother's funeral. The place was a wreck. He'd worked for the previous owner many years before. He put in that stone walk." He pointed at the path to the house.

Pablo stared at the flat, gray stones, laid with precision and artfulness. They were the only physical traces he had seen of his father since his mother had left him. He studied the stones as if they could reveal the man. A hard, neat worker, there was no question of that. Someone who worked close to the soil. A laborer. A touch of the artist.

"He said he'd be back in the fall," the man said, "but he never came."

There was a troubled expression on the woman's face as she turned to her husband. "The storage building," she said. He looked surprised, as if suddenly remembering, and nodded. Then she turned to Pablo. "A canvas bag," she said. "He forgot it when he left for Texas. We thought he'd be back."

The man turned and headed toward a low, flat building to the side of the house. His wife followed. Then the man looked over his shoulder and beckoned to Pablo.

* * *

They were retired schoolteachers from California who had come to this quiet place to write and paint. The woman fed Pablo breakfast over his embarrassed protests that he was not hungry. It was the first American breakfast he had eaten since Santa Fe. When they asked him if he wanted to stay a while and work, he shook his head. He had to get back. He placed the lunch that the woman packed for him in the canvas bag and headed for the village.

It was there, on the trail, finally alone, that he gave in to his emotions. He sat in the shade of a tree and unzipped the canvas bag with "Dallas Cowboys" in faded printing on the side, a worn out companion to his visored cap. He started to weep, wondering what else he and his father might have had in common. Inside the bag were a few clues: a pair of worn leather work gloves, a photograph in a cardboard folder of a woman—not his mother—with three small children standing beside her, a well-used paperback Spanish-English dictionary, and a plaid woolen shirt with holes in the elbows. Not much of a legacy to leave to a son and even less if shared with three other children.

When he finally reached the village, Pablo went directly to El Jefe, who sat as before on a wooden chair leaning against the wall of his casita. "I found this," Pablo said, holding up the canvas bag. "And this," handing El Jefe the cardboard folder.

The old eyes squinted, staring hard at the photograph. "She's not from here," he finally said, handing it back.

"They told me he had gone to Texas but never returned." The old man looked at Pablo, and it was as if a shadow had passed across his face. "Do you know anything about Texas?" Pablo asked.

The old man looked away and sat thoughtfully. "Verónica!" he shouted. A ragged little girl popped out from behind the casita. "Go bring your grandmother!"

Soon the little girl came skipping back with the old woman who had met Pablo on the trail. "Yes, Jefe."

"Texas," he said. "There was something about Texas."

"There are lots of things about Texas." The old woman sounded annoyed.

"About Ramón Barreras," El Jefe said. "Something I can't remember." The old woman shook her head. "Try!" El Jefe said.

The old woman sighed in exasperation. "I remember— they said he was going to Texas."

"Bah!" The old man spit into the dirt. "We already know that."

She closed her eyes and rubbed a thumb and forefinger up and down on the bridge of her nose. "He never came back," she finally said, opening her eyes.

"Bah!"

"And there was a rumor . . ."

"Yes!" El Jefe said.

The old woman looked at Pablo, weighing what it was she was about to reveal. "Someone said . . . that he had . . . died in Texas." Pablo looked at the canvas bag that lay at his feet. Her words shocked him even though he should have expected them. Hadn't his dream told him that he was dying? "It was only a rumor," the old woman said. "Nobody knew for certain."

"But he never came back," Pablo said.

The old woman nodded and made the sign of the cross.

* * *

When he went to the highway to wait for the bus, an Indian couple was standing by the roadside waiting patiently. The Indian, old enough to be Pablo's father, stared admiringly at his Dallas Cowboys cap.

Pablo nodded and sat in the shade. "At what hour does the bus come?" he asked. The Indian shook his head that he didn't know.

Sitting there drowsily, Pablo began to feel that he was being watched. He turned but saw nothing. He slid the canvas bag up against his side and kept his hand on it. He shook his head, then slapped his cheeks to keep awake, to keep from dreaming.

Later, on the bus, Pablo stared out the window, thinking he might see a familiar white figure loping across the country-side alongside them. "If I just keep awake," he said to himself, "everything will be all right."

For some reason, like on the trip from Juárez, he did not dream while traveling. At each stop though, he closely watched the boarding passengers, wary that he might see a familiar face. But it was at the end of the journey, in the Juárez station, when it happened. As he alighted from the bus, straw and canvas bags in hand, he heard a voice from the crowd.

"Joven. Young man. You're back so soon. Don't you like our country?"

Pablo gripped his bags tighter and turned away. As he pushed through the crowd, he heard the hoarse, accented voice right behind him.

"Young man, Juan Zorro at your service."

Then the man was alongside him, knowing eyes above a crooked smile. He took the cigarette from his mouth and coughed quickly and politely to the side. Pablo recognized him even though his dyed hair was fading so that there were streaks of white shot through the black. On the man's left lobe was a small silver skull, an earring, that he hadn't noticed before. Pablo shivered because there was something else about the man; he thought he recognized him from his dreams.

"You have your papers so you can go back to the Northland of Millionaires?" When Pablo looked puzzled, the man said, "Proof that you're really a Norteamericano? Birth certificate. Passport. Tourist card."

"But I'm an American!" the startled Pablo said.

"Look at yourself in the mirror. You think La Migra is going to believe you—a brownskin, underage boy?"

"But I speak English."

"So do I, joven. That's not enough."

Pablo tried to remember what he carried in his wallet. He did not want to bring it out in front of this—this—he could not bring himself to think the word: coyote.

"I—I have my Social Security card!" Pablo said, feeling relief that he had some proof.

Juan Zorro grinned. "I print those up by the hundred," he said. "I even carry one myself. But . . ." He shook his head, showing that it was next to useless.

Pablo stopped at the corner bewildered, trying to think through what he had just been told. He had never thought about getting back into Los Estados Unidos. It had been so easy to get into Mexico. He thought it would be the same going back.

Juan Zorro lit another cigarette from the dying embers of the stub from which he had just taken the last puff. He blew smoke from the new cigarette out of the side of his mouth away from Pablo.

"Listen, joven," Juan Zorro said. "If you go over the bridge you need papers: proof of citizenship, work permit, tourist card, something. You can speak all the English you want, but without papers, they won't let you across. I can help you. How much money you got?"

Pablo shook his head. "No money, no papers," Juan Zorro said. "You got three bucks?"

Pablo stood still, not shaking his head, thinking. Juan Zorro smiled his crooked smile. "That's all you need," he said. "Just tres dólares. I can meet you at the place tonight. Furnish transportation across. It's a perfect night. No moon. You're as good as home."

Pablo was so surprised that it only cost three dollars that he almost paid the man in advance. At three in the morning he sat on the bank of the Río Bravo listening to the flow of the water and waiting. Later he heard whispered voices from behind the shrubbery, other pilgrims waiting to cross to the promised land.

Shortly before dawn he heard the sound of a truck in the distance and the bushes began to rustle. He made out dim figures in the dark moving in a line along the bank of the river. "Por aquí," someone off to the side whispered. Pablo rose and followed.

"Dinero," he heard the rasping voice of Juan Zorro whisper. "Tres dólares." There was the sound of something up ahead moving into the water. Then Pablo was at the front of the line.

"Ah," came the hoarse whisper. "My young friend. Dinero. Tres dólares."

Juan Zorro added the three bills to the stack in his hand. "Here," Juan Zorro said. "Guaranteed to get you safely across."

Pablo took the oversize inner tube. He ran his hand along a bump of patches on one side and squeezed to make sure it didn't leak. "Don't worry," Juan Zorro said. "It's perfectly safe. Come on. I'll launch you myself."

Juan Zorro stuffed the bills into his pocket and motioned his head for a companion to take over.

"Dinero," the companion chanted in a whisper. "Tres dólares."

Pablo followed Juan Zorro upstream. He could hear the splashing of water and see dim outlines paddling their way across.

"Here," Juan Zorro said. He took the inner tube from Pablo and dropped it in the water. "Now sit. It doesn't matter that your ass gets wet. At least you won't be a wetback." And he rasped what could have been a laugh or a cough.

Pablo set his bags on the ground and waded out to the tube held steady by Juan Zorro. He sat in the hole, his feet dangling over one end, his hands lightly grasping the sides. Then, before he knew what was happening, Juan Zorro pushed the tube out into the river and gave it a strong shove into the current.

"Paddle with your hands!" Juan Zorro shouted. "Don't let the current carry you too far!"

"My bags!" Pablo shouted, watching in dismay as the land receded.

"Don't worry!" came the distant shout. "I'll take care of them!" Then the rasp that Pablo now knew was laughter.

My things! he thought. My inheritance! My birthright! Papá, forgive me!

He was picking up speed, moving what he thought must be south, and he realized that he had better paddle to get across. He took one last look toward Mexico. There on the bank of the river, sitting on its haunches, was a large white coyote grinning at him. He shook his head in disbelief, and when he looked again, the coyote was gone.

* * *

Pablo hadn't been in the river long when he heard voices floating on the water. They were old-timers having a conversation as if over the dinner table, discussing the merits of their inner tubes and whether or not they had paid the best price. "We should get a discount for crossing so often," one of the men said.

Pablo paddled harder, following the voices until the current slowed, then stopped altogether. He saw the men scramble up the bank and disappear.

It was still early morning when Pablo found the place he had slept that first night in El Paso. He crawled under a cover of shrubbery and fell asleep, exhausted.

"There is no border," a voice said in his dream.

It took a moment for him to realize that it was his own voice. That there was no white coyote leering at him. Then, with a flutter of wings, the black crow landed beside him.

"He told me that there is no border," Pablo said. "That it's all one land."

"Then why did you pay him to sneak you back across the river?" the crow asked.

"But the land looks the same on both sides."

"Tell that to La Migra," the crow said. "Borders can be what anyone says they are."

Pablo stared at the bird, not knowing what to say. "Well," he finally said, "it's good to be going home."

"One must live where one belongs," the crow said. "I can hardly wait to get back to my piñón country." Then he looked at Pablo, and if crows' beaks bent and smiled, he would have smiled. "There is a border of the soul, Chicanito. You can only be at peace when you find the right place, no matter how hard things may be."

The crow ruffled its feathers, then spread its wings to test them before flapping to the top of the shrub. "I'm on my way," the crow said. "Hasta la vista."

"Hasta la vista."

Then his dream became sound. The whir of tires on asphalt. Reba McEntire singing, this time about a new fool at an old game. He could see the highway rising, the landscape turning green, and the piñón trees waiting to welcome him back.

FAMILY THANKSGIVING

I never understood why Mamá insisted on living in that little adobe house in the country that was left to her by her mother. I do know that when Papá died, she sold their house in town because it was haunted by too many sad memories. She also needed the money to pay medical bills. At the same time, her widowed mother, my Grandma Sánchez, was alone and starting to fade. Grandma's chickens were bones and feathers because she sometimes forgot to feed them. The nanny goat's udder had gone dry, and she was only fit to barbeque—if you could stand ribs without much meat on them. Furthermore, the vegetable garden had been overrun by a ragtag army of weeds.

I had a suspicion that Mamá felt compelled to be a nurse, although she complained about Grandma Sánchez the same way she complained about working in an office in town. Yet when I told her I'd help pay for a part-time housekeeper, she blew up.

"I'm going to do my duty to my mother, Irene," she said. "And I don't care what you think." I was just part of an entire generation of selfish young people, she raved on. She didn't have to read about the "me" generation in the newspapers to know. All she had to do was look at her own children.

"Fine," I said. "Do you complain because you overwork? Or do you overwork so you can complain?" For an instant I thought she was going to smack me.

Instead she said that she liked New Mexico country. It reminded her of when she was a girl. Quiet and slow. Peaceful. A retreat from the crazy city life people lived today. She could look at the house and take pride that her father and uncles had built it adobe brick by adobe brick almost fifty years ago. It connected her to her roots. Adobe was cool in the summer and warm in the winter. Her garden was a constant delight, both to work in and to harvest. Besides, where better for her children and grandchildren to gather on important occasions? Like Thanksgiving.

Of course she didn't reckon with the families of her two sons-in-law and one daughter-in-law. As far as Mamá was concerned, other families were a supporting cast back in the shadows. But I could hear my sisters' husbands grousing to my brother, Dan, that they had to spend Christmas with their parents this year. Dan was the only one not drinking beer. He had to go on duty right after dinner. His neatly pressed police officer's uniform was hanging in Mamá's bedroom closet.

"Hey, big sister Reeny," Dan said when I carried out a stack of plates to the living room. He and little brother Sammy had lugged the plastic-top table from the kitchen to where things were being set up buffet style. "What's this I hear about you defending those Commies?"

"What Commies?" I knew damn well what he meant: the sanctuary defendants.

"The wetback smugglers."

"What smugglers?" I answered.

"All right, be that way." He cast an envious glance at his brothers-in-law's beer cans, ignoring the silly grins on their faces. I didn't. They were waiting for me to pop off and start the show.

"Reeny," Dan went on. "Why didn't you stay with the district attorney's office? How come you became a public defender for that low-life you deal with in court? Jesus!"

I couldn't stand it. Members of your family really know where to get you. I set the plates on the table and shot my right arm straight out in a salute. "Heil, Hitler!"

The goofball brothers-in-law started to snicker. Dan glowered at them. Then he turned back to me. "I ought to know better than to ask."

Little Sammy, bless his heart, started to recite some lines from the play he was rehearsing. He did the voices of all the characters, starting out with Jacob Marley, answering as the Ghost of Christmas Past, and ending as Tiny Tim blessing everyone.

I retreated to the kitchen to keep from giving Dan another shot, the ingrate. When I had been with the D.A.'s office I had helped tutor him for his police exam. Obviously I hadn't tutored him well enough about being innocent until proven guilty.

Mamá had gone next door to borrow a cup of something or other. If I know her, she was probably spreading it on pretty thick about her loving family that was with her this holiday. Especially if it was old lady Cordova whose children didn't even speak to her anymore.

My youngest sister, Lisa, was basting the turkey. "Where's Marta?" I asked.

"Cleaning up after the kids." Since Marta had three children, Lisa two, and Dan and Helen only one, I guess child messes were more Marta's problem. "If one more little brat spills anything on the floor I think I'll scream." The spoon in Lisa's hand was shaking.

"Here. Let me do that," I said.

What I wanted to tell her was to have a beer or a glass of the Chablis that Sammy brought. Sammy was the one in the family with a little class. But even when she wasn't uptight, Lisa wouldn't take a drink. She figured if she did, her husband would have an excuse to be like his father and drink even more, although a couple of beers on holidays was no big deal as far as I was concerned.

Her arms were folded across her chest as she watched me. "Are you taking Mother to mass this Christmas?" There was a hard edge to her voice. It was an unnecessary question since she already knew the answer. She was probably pissed off because her husband was having a good time watching the football game on TV and laughing and scratching with the other changos.

I closed the oven door and put the spoon on the counter. "I think the turkey's almost ready," I said.

"Are you?" she insisted.

Oh, Lord, I thought. What is it about me that brings out the worst in my family? Is it because I'm the oldest? Am I so different? Was I born into the wrong tribe?

Luckily Marta and Helen came in just then. "I sent them all out," Marta said. "Little María's in charge. Nobody gets back in before dinner unless they're bleeding." She picked an open beer can off the counter and drained it as she eyed us. "What's with you two?"

"Nothing," I said.

"Hmm."

"I think we should heat up the chiles rellenos," I said. They were Mamá's specialty. The old-fashioned kind with green chili and beef ground really fine, garnished with raisins, and shaped like short, fat Chinese egg rolls. Mamá always heated Log Cabin syrup to pour over them for a sweet and hot Southwestern dish that was really a treat.

"She's not taking Mother to mass again this Christmas," Lisa said.

"Why don't *you* then?" Marta said. Then she looked at me with a mischievous smile on her face. "Tell me, Reeny. Are you going to marry Robert?"

Robert was a student counselor at the local high school. Marta's husband, Leo, who was a teacher at the same school, had accidentally-on-purpose invited Robert over one night when I came for dinner. I used to think that it was only unhappily married relatives who couldn't stand to see one of their kin single. Especially divorced older sisters who were pushing forty. But Marta and Leo were a pretty good match, which disproved that theory.

"Are you kidding?" I said. Helen suddenly got busy carrying the good stainless flatware to the living room. I figured she and Dan had been over that subject more than a few times.

"He's hot to marry you. He even told Mamá when she was over one night." Well, goody-goody, I thought. It's none of Mamá's business. Marta had a funny expression on her face. Maybe she had read my mind. "Has he ever asked you?"

"Oh, yeah."

That look was still on her face. She popped open a fresh beer can and took a swallow. "Has he ever been married?" I shook my head. "God, he's got to be almost forty. Is—is he—normal? You know what I mean. Not—"

I almost laughed. "He's just an old-fashioned boy. When his papá died he promised to take care of his mamá the rest of her life. The old bag is going to live to be a hundred."

"You sure he's not—you know—gay?"

"You're not worried about Leo, are you?" I asked.

Marta hooted. "Oh, really!" Lisa said indignantly. Helen, who had come back, looked shocked.

All three of them were watching me closely, eager to know what was none of their business. "Well," I said, "one night we went out to dinner and he asked me to marry him. I told him he didn't have to marry me if all he wanted was to go to bed."

"This is disgusting," Lisa said, and stomped into the living room.

"He'd just have to ask me some night when I wasn't exhausted from work," I continued. "He almost choked on his steak. His face got red right up to the roots of his hair." Marta was laughing. Helen's mouth fell open. "Have you ever seen Dan blush?" I asked Helen.

She shook her head slowly, staring at me as if I was the kind of woman her sweet old mother had warned her about.

"I don't think my brother can," I said. "Not even if his pants dropped to his ankles in the middle of mass."

Marta was having a fit by now; there were tears in her eyes from laughing so hard.

Dan came in with that cocky streetwalk of his that I call the Aztec strut. "What're you hens cackling about?"

"Oh, go back with the boys and play with your drumstick," I said.

Marta and I looked at each other and started to giggle as we did when we were girls. Helen looked from us to her husband as if she didn't know what to do.

The screen door creaked open and Mamá came up the back steps into the kitchen. Her eyes were shiny, as if she had just seen an apparition of the Virgin in the backyard, and she was smiling. The large bowl in her hand was full of ice cubes.

"It's such a blessing to see my family having such a good time," Mamá said.

"Hey, give me that," Dan said, taking the bowl and putting it into the refrigerator. "You should have told me you wanted ice. I could have gone to the liquor store for a bag."

"You children always had such a good time together," Mamá said. "Never a fuss. Never a harsh word."

Marta and I exchanged glances as we did when we were children and Mamá insisted that there really was a Santa Claus even after we had snooped all over the house and finally found the presents in the broom closet.

"I put the rellenos on to heat," I said. "The turkey is ready to come out."

"Everything's ready out here," Lisa hollered from the front room.

"All right," Mamá said. "I guess it's time. Don't forget to turn off the stove," she said to Marta. "And call the children," she said to Helen.

We went into the front room and gathered around the niche with the plaster statue of Jesus pointing to his sacred heart. It was across the room from the niche with the photo of Papá in his army uniform. Lisa hissed at the men to get rid of their beer cans.

Mamá lit the two votives as we shuffled restlessly in a cluster, leaving enough room for her and the kids to kneel. The rest of us stood. "All right, Daniel," she said. "You can begin now."

Lisa stared at my motionless right hand as she made a sign of the cross. Dan began to recite a prayer out loud, and the others joined in. He ended saying grace, and I joined this time. Then the line formed at the end of the loaded table. Dan began to carve the turkey while Sammy turned up the sound on the TV.

I got out of the way of the stampede and went out the front door to get some fresh air and wait for the line to shorten. Marta sneaked out after me. We picked our way through the chickens away from the house.

"Did you really say that to Robert?" she asked in a low voice. "About going to bed?" I just smiled without answering. After all, I had my reputation to uphold. "You're just teasing, aren't you?" she said. "You're always teasing."

"How come you're not inside feeding the kids?"

"It's Lisa's turn."

From inside, her oldest daughter María's voice sang out, "Rub-a-dub-dub. Thanks for the grub. Yea, God!"

I looked at Marta. Well, I thought. Now there'll be hell to pay. They'll probably blame that on me, too. But it didn't bother Marta at all. She sort of squinted and stared into my eyes as if she was trying to see inside me. "Are you going to marry Robert?"

I put a hand on her arm. "No," I said. "He's a lovely man but there's just nothing there. If there's no spark, why bother?"

"Mamá will have a conniption. She practically had the wedding planned."

"Maybe we should fix her up with Robert. Older women and younger men are in these days."

Marta wasn't sure whether or not to take me seriously. When I smiled, she started to giggle. Then Lisa pushed open the screen door. I half expected her to say something about little María, but all she said was, "Come and get it!"

Be thankful for little things, I thought. Now all I needed was Dan to rush out with a plate in his hand saying that he was late for work and that we would argue about my Commie clients some other time. If I had really believed in prayer I would have prayed for that right then. But all that came to me was : Rub-a-dub-dub. Thanks for the grub. Yea—

RADIO WAVES

María was in the kitchen making breakfast noises. Then the radio waves came again and told Bobby what to do. Right out of the air.

"I want my cereal!" he yelled. He pounded on the table with his spoon. "Bring me my cereal!"

María came to the door between the kitchen and the dining room. She had on her uniform. She was brown, and her face was young and smooth. She cooked OK for a housekeeper. She was nice when Mother and Father weren't home. Brown was the color of nice.

"Stop that, honey," María said. "You'll scratch the table."

But the signals hadn't stopped so he had to keep pounding. "Bobby, I'll have to tell your mother and father." She didn't sound as if she meant it.

Her face was worried, and her voice was worried. But she wasn't in control. The radio waves were.

"I don't care!" he yelled. "I want my cereal!"

The radio waves must have spoken to her too. She sighed and went back into the kitchen. He kept pounding. "Here," she said when she came back.

"I want the one with cinnamon and raisins," Bobby said.

"Corn flakes are good for you."

But he kept pounding, and she left. When she came back she had the box with the colored picture of cinnamon and raisins on it.

The radio waves told him it was OK to put down the spoon. "How do you spell cinnamon?" he asked.

She sighed again. She always sighed. "C . . . I . . . N . . ."

"All right. All right," he said, waving his hand excitedly. He could see the word on the box. ". . . N . . . A . . . M . . . O . . . N."

Bobby looked up, but she didn't smile. Didn't he get it right?

"Now eat your cereal," she said. "Your mother and father will be right down. They stayed on purpose just to see you. They're on a tight schedule."

They were always on a tight schedule.

Bobby could tell by the sound that it was Mother walking. "Good morning, Bobby," she said. She was in a hurry and breathless, as if she was unsure of him.

"Beep, beep," he said.

She gave María a funny look. "Just coffee, María." Then she looked at Bobby. "Don't touch my make-up," she said. "I don't have time to redo it. Well," she said, "what are we this morning?"

"Beep, beep, beep."

Bobby put down his spoon and slid off the chair. He started to walk around the table. He could do it with his legs stiff. His left arm swung forward when he took a step with his left leg. The same with his right arm and his right leg.

"That's not normal," Mother said, frowning.

"Beep, beep."

Bobby started to walk that way fast. Round and round the table.

"Stop that," Mother said. She sounded scared.

"Beep."

Then the heavy footsteps came into the room. The radio waves told him to walk faster, faster.

"For Christ's sakes," Father said. "What the hell is it this morning?"

"Beep, beep, beep."

"Stop that this instant, young man!"

"Beep." Bobby went faster, faster.

"María!" Mother yelled. "Is there room for Dr. Margolis on Bobby's schedule?"

"Yes, ma'am."

Then Father said something in his gringo-accented Spanish, and María looked at Bobby and nodded.

The radio waves sent him another message. This time when Bobby came around by his chair, he reached over and turned the cereal bowl upside down. The milk ran out from under the edge of the bowl, along the table, and onto the carpet.

"Goddamn it!" Father yelled. "He's driving me crazy."

Bobby thought that Mother was going to cry, but her cold eyes just got red.

"I'll clean it up," María said.

"This can't go on," Father said. "You know I have to fly to Boston today for the computer conference."

"Well, I can't take off work," Mother said. "I'm in charge of the new campaign for the bank. Today is the deadline for our first ad."

"Beep," Bobby said.

María was leaning over, cleaning the tabletop. "Demonio," she said when Bobby bumped into her.

"María," Mother said. "Call Dr. Margolis's office. Maybe they can squeeze him in early. Maybe Doctor can give him . . . something."

"Beep."

Bobby thought really hard and told the radio waves that his legs and arms were getting tired. They signaled him back. He slowed and threw himself at Mother, holding her tight.

"Bobby," she said. "Please. You'll wrinkle me."

Then Father grabbed him under the arms, but Bobby wouldn't let go.

"Stop it, Bobby!" Mother yelled. "You're messing my suit!"

The radio waves told him to let go. Father held him really hard. It hurt. Father carried him from the dining room to the other room. The empty one. He shoved Bobby inside. Bobby lay on the floor kicking. He could hear the key turn in the lock.

After a while Bobby crept to the door and listened through the keyhole.

"And to think that I made myself late just to see him," Mother said. "Let me take the Mercedes today. You'd just be parked in the airport lot the rest of the week anyway."

"María," Father said, "don't forget to phone Margolis right away."

"María," Mother said, "I'll be late again tonight."

* * *

The doctor's office was in a tall building near the university. The sign said Children's Hospital/Psychiatry. Dr. Margolis's office was on the fourth floor. They rode up on the elevator. Bobby drew away from María when a nurse boarded on the second floor.

"Well," Dr. Margolis's nurse said when they entered. "Aren't we the little man. That's a very handsome suit you're wearing. Your parents certainly take good care of you."

"Buzz," he replied.

"The doctor will be with you in a minute," the nurse said to María. "He's about finished with his nine o'clock appointment."

Bobby sat stiffly on one of the child-size chairs. He looked at the pile of children's books and magazines on the little table.

"Here," María said, handing him a coloring book. He picked up a brown crayon and neatly filled in the smiling face on one of the pages. Then he took the red crayon, holding it like a dagger, and colored deep red gouges across the opposite page. He held the coloring book out at arm's length and dropped it onto the floor. María frowned.

The nurse smiled and called Bobby. "Now be nice to Doctor," María whispered.

"Buzz," he said.

He closed his eyes for a second and listened for the radio waves, but they hardly ever followed him into the doctor's office. When he reached the office he waited for the nurse to open the door.

"Well, there you are," Dr. Margolis said. "Come in, Bobby."

He sat in the little chair, and Doctor sat in the big chair. There was a low table between them.

"Have you been to school this morning?" Doctor asked.

"Buzz."

Doctor looked at him solemnly. Doctor understood. He sat very still, looking at Bobby. Maybe he could hear the radio waves too. Only the radio waves hardly ever came into Doctor's office.

"Let's *pretend* you're in school instead," Doctor said. He handed Bobby a thin little book. "Read the first part of this. Then we'll talk about it. I have to leave for a moment." Bobby took the book that Doctor had opened to page one. "You can read it, can't you?"

"Buzz, buzz," Bobby said. Doctor's face relaxed, and he smiled.

"Dick and Jane live in a white house," Bobby read. "Mother wears an apron and bakes cookies. Dick and Jane like cookies. Father goes to the city to work. Dick and Jane wave goodbye. They have a dog named Spot. Spot barks goodbye."

Bobby slammed the book shut and threw it across the room. The door opened a crack. "That's only the second time they've seen him this week?" Doctor said.

"Yes, sir," María said. She sounded like she was crying. "But I can't do anything about it."

"Does he still talk to you in words?"

"Yes, sir. Most of the time."

Then Doctor must have realized that the door was open because the door clicked shut. Bobby went to where the book lay on the floor. He picked it up and threw it at the wall. When he turned back toward his little chair, Doctor was standing with his hand on the doorknob watching him.

"What does your friend, Gort, say when you throw books?" Doctor asked. Bobby shook his head but didn't utter a sound. "Does he go 'buzz'?" Bobby didn't answer. He walked to the little chair, sat down, and closed his eyes.

"Doesn't Gort like to talk when you throw books?"

Bobby closed his eyes tighter and put his hands over his ears. Only he wouldn't be able to hear any radio waves with his ears covered.

After a few minutes, his hands got tired, and he relaxed them. Now he was at the seashore. The ocean hissed as if through a seashell. Then he heard the scratching. That would be Doctor writing in his notebook. When he heard the clunk, Bobby opened his eyes a crack. The crayons and blank paper were on the table in front of him. He closed his eyes tightly and pressed his hands over his ears again.

Something bumped against his chair. He felt a large arm lie softly across his shoulder. A large hand began to pat him.

"Aiii . . . iii . . . iiiiii!" Bobby screamed. The tears ran out of his closed eyes onto his cheeks. "Aiiiiiiiiiiii!"

The hand kept patting his back. His throat got scratchy and hot. He finally stopped screaming. His hands were tired again, and he let them fall to his lap.

After a minute Doctor said, "I'll get you some orange juice for your throat."

Silence. Bobby slowly sipped the juice and dropped the empty paper cup on the carpet. Doctor opened the box of crayons and spread them out on the table.

"Draw me a picture," Doctor said. Bobby stared at the paper and at all the colors. "Go ahead," Doctor said. "You don't have to talk. Just draw. Anything you want."

After a little while, Bobby rubbed his eyes dry and reached for the red crayon. He held it in his little fist as if it was a dagger and pressed hard on the paper, stabbing deep, thick, angry red lines over and over in the center of the page. Then he put the red crayon in his pocket and picked up the black crayon. Once again he wielded his dagger, grinding black into the lower right corner of the paper. On the upper left corner he tapped the point of the crayon very softly to make a lone little black dot. He threw the black crayon across the room.

"Now draw another one," Doctor said.

Bobby was still looking at the colors when the door opened. "Your next patient is here, Doctor," the nurse said.

María came in. Bobby stood without a word. Doctor handed María a little brown bottle that she put in her purse. "Like I said before—" Doctor's voice was low. "Crush and dissolve two in fruit juice at meals and bedtime."

Bobby was the first to leave by the side door, the one that didn't go past the waiting room. "And you tell them," Doctor said, "that one of them has to be here next week. I don't care which one."

"Yes, sir."

María took Bobby's hand as they walked down the hall. "You don't have to go to school today if you don't want to," she said kindly. She sounded like her regular self now. The everyday María. The one he knew when his mother and father weren't around. But it was too late.

Bobby was starting to feel sleepy. The tight muscles in his back started to loosen, like when Doctor rubbed them. His eyes felt heavy. He wanted to close them and listen for the radio waves, but they were already at the elevator. You didn't shut your eyes in the elevator. That could take you down, down below the first floor to the devil's room.

The door slid open, and they stepped in. A nurse in white smiled at them. Bobby shook María's hand away. He felt so tired. So tired. He didn't even want María.

"Are you all right?" María whispered when the door opened on the first floor.

"Plink," he said.

There had been a catch in her voice, almost a cry. Her eyes turned red, and now he could see the streaks down her cheeks where tears had washed the face powder from her brown face.

"Are you all right?" she whispered again as they walked to the parking lot.

"Plink."

* * *

When they finally got home, Bobby took off his suit coat and dropped it on the floor.

"I'll make you a nice early lunch," María said. "Grilled cheese and tomato soup. Your favorite."

"Plink."

He heard the radio waves now that he was home, and they were loud. Louder than they had ever been before. It happened right after he passed the bulletin board where his mother and father tacked the notes for María. They were his schedule, Gort told him over the radio waves. The message center that controlled his life. There was no need to talk. The radio waves would say everything. If other people couldn't hear, that was their tough luck. They didn't belong in his life.

Bobby walked into the other room, the empty room. He closed the door and sat on the rug, staring at the bare white wall. There was a soft tap on the closed door. "Bobby, are you all right?"

"Plink," he said. But he didn't say it very loud. He wanted to listen instead. They were coming again, louder and louder. Beep. Buzz. Plink. And much, much more.